OVERSIGHT

D1739252

THOMAS CLABURN

For Andrea, Catia, and Tasha.

CHAPTER ONE

OVERSIGHT

SPECTACLES LIE ASKEW on the dead man's face. Sam notices the delicate frames before the gore and absence of eyes. Hate he's seen in abundance, but rarely rose-colored glasses.

The others share his detachment. It's early still; morning fog masks the steam from coffee cups. In the mist, men in uniforms laugh among themselves, their insular mirth echoed by unseen gulls. In the city, the sound would be sirens. Here in the Marin Headlands, the dead sleep well.

Sam misses the luxury of sleep. Downtime doesn't pay the bills. Information does. Sam Crane is a data speculator. He makes his living documenting infidelity, mostly. He dabbles in corporate intelligence too, but has enough sense to sell evidence only on the most trivial infractions; meaningful revelations can get you sued or killed. Specs almost never get prosecuted, but it is a possibility. The epic scope of the criminal code ensures that everyone has broken the law, and thus can be arrested when convenient.

A car passes, slowing just enough for the occupants to rubberneck.

Techs in clean suits are pecking the ground for biological evidence. With their long-necked vacuums stretched out in front of them, they seem to be walking invisible dogs. Silk flowers and simulated grass—the National Parking Service's bandage for the blighted landscape—crackle beneath their boots. The smell of plastic undermines the illusion.

A moon-faced man with a goatee is directing the operation, straight-handled umbrella tucked firmly under his arm, dark hair disciplined with pomade. He wears a month's pay in the form of a designer suit. Luis Cisco is the captain of one the more able homicide crews in the San Francisco area. It's been a year since Sam last saw him, over beers at the ballpark.

"Watch your step," Luis says.

Sam climbs down into the drainage ditch and takes a closer look at the corpse. An older man. Out of shape. Soft and easily cut.

Gingerly, with hands gloved in latex, he lifts the spectacles. Two wires, candy-cane twisted, form the temples, each of which terminates in a button-sized copper disk. A single wire defines each oval frame. The pink glass lenses are both intact.

"His glasses are in remarkably good shape considering there are two holes where his eyes used to be," Sam says. "Hardly an accident, I think."

"Meet Dr. Xian Mako."

"An eye doctor?"

Luis tames his grin. "An apparently unemployed PhD."

"He's not listed?"

"There's nothing about him in any of the public databases."

"You get what you pay for," Sam observes, knowing how much Luis hates being made to feel cheap.

"We found portions of a list that had been posted by the Animal Legal Fund in 2046. There was a picture of him that matched the image we sent out."

"Tagged?"

"It was. We found his name, degree, and affiliation in the metadata. We searched and got one relevant hit in the GeneTrak database. But apart from his name, all form fields were blank. Not even a valid home address. Interested?"

"I answered your call, didn't I?" Sam stands and wipes the grit from his jeans. "You seem anxious to hand this one off, Luis. Not even gonna wait for the results of the vid and vac?"

Luis gestures with his umbrella, cutting an arc through the air. "Take a look around. That's not dust. It's skin and hair. The slough of a thousand felons. I'd have better luck matching a sample with the floor sweepings in my hair salon."

"I'm sure you meant to say 'barber shop.'"

Luis clucks derisively. "You get what you pay for."

"Don't like my buzz?"

"You look like a Q-tip."

"People tell me it looks good."

"What people?"

"This girl I've been seeing."

Luis smirks. "You must be paying her well."

Fists tightening, Sam forces a smile and turns his attention back to the corpse on the ground. "Nowhere near what you seem to be earning with your moonlighting." Seeing Luis bristle, he backs off. "Genetic decoys are the mark of a professional hit. I'll probably end up chasing my own tail."

"You'd be doing me a favor."

"Does this mean you've given up on the Solve-O-Matic?"

"No," Luis says, eyes downcast, "there's no way I can make my quota without it. And it actually does well if you have some leads. But I like to throw a bit of work to you specs now and again."

"As much as I'd like to play John Henry to your steam drill, I need more."

"You want me to beg? I can't afford another red name on my board."

Sam grins. "It'd serve you right being busted back to desk duty." He jerks his thumb at the middle-aged man in a jogging suit waiting by the side of the road. "Did that guy see anything?"

"No such luck. Albert Bear. He found the body."

"I take it the professor left no funds for an inquiry?"

"Basically. His testamentary file forbids payment for posthumous legal services. He wants to be cremated, no autopsy. Everything goes to a charity for compulsive shoppers. The file is suspiciously scant."

"You think it's been altered?"

"Maybe I'm just being paranoid."

"Well, if he didn't want an autopsy, he shouldn't have gotten himself killed. You gonna pick up the tab for that?"

"Yeah," Luis says ruefully. "Should've never answered the call."

Sam looks more closely at the glasses. "Do the initials 'J.M.' mean anything to you? They're engraved on the frame."

Luis shakes his head. The rustling of the leaves sounds wrong.

"You know, there's no registration mark," Sam observes, holding the spectacles up to the sky. "No bothersome licensing restrictions to prevent resale."

"Always a bad idea to sell evidence."

"Unless the price is right. Anyway, it might pique someone's interest. Mind if I borrow them?"

Luis shrugs. "If you're signed on as the lead, fine. You lose them and it's your head, not mine."

Sam pulls the glove from his right hand. "Sure, but next funded case, you bring me in for half. Deal?"

"You know I can't do that. Thirty percent gets kicked back to the city. That leaves next to nothing for my crew and me." Luis brushes a wayward hair from the collar of his designer jacket. "My operating costs are not insignificant."

"Half of your net, then."

Hesitating, Luis grasps Sam's hand and shakes in a way that feels non-committal. "If you close this case."

"I do the work. You get the credit."

"It's the way of the world, Sam."

Sam pockets the glasses, zips his leather jacket, and returns to his motorcycle on the far side of the road. It's a turn-of-the-century Ducati, worn but still vital. He guns the engine to hear it sing. Environmental restrictions have silenced newer-model engines, but this bike's voice reminds him of Louis Armstrong.

Crossing the gridlocked Golden Gate Bridge beneath a swath of fog, Sam addresses his network agent using his helmet mic. "Marilyn, find files on Dr. Xian Mako. Include pay-per-view databases in query. Bid up to $100 per result. Stop at ten. Log listings above that number for future review. Accept signed barter deals if requested data valued at $120 or less exists in my sale directory. Copy results to my private directory at GeoSync Five. Authorize by voice."

Marilyn Monroe's voice coos, "Your request has been received, Sam. You sound like you could use some rest. How would you like a weekend in Hawaii? Air West is now offering flights from $3999."

The network's voice recognition routine invariably mistakes Sam's rasp—tuned by cigarettes and exhaust—for fatigue or ill health. He's been targeted with so many medicinal pitches that he's beginning to wonder if he might actually be sick.

He dials down the sound in his helmet. The volume control is forbidden by the terms of his helmet-licensing agreement, but it's a necessity. Many people have a dentonator implanted in a tooth for audio transmission. But those are even worse; they're specially designed to be difficult to turn off—and they make the wearer easy to track. Buying silence is, of course, always an option, but it's an expensive habit.

Seemingly random lane closures on the bridge achieve

their intended effect, slowing traffic to maximize exposure to projected commercials that seem to play out in the air between bridge cables. Sam tries to keep his eyes on the road instead. After fifteen minutes, he decides to snake, despite the shakedown fines. Dozens of traffic complaints will be waiting for him when he gets home, courtesy of those he's passed. The slighted drivers will get a dollar each, though they'll be obliged to pay thirty percent to the city. That much money wouldn't buy time from a parking meter, but it's enough to pay down his debt to society.

The fog over the waterfront burns away. Across the bay, Oakland basks in sunlight beneath broken clouds. Sam speeds south on Third Street past soulless Mission Bay apartments toward the last bastion of industrial San Francisco, Hunter's Point. Old warehouses huddle there, defying the encroachment of Kava Man and Tube Burger franchises.

Maerskton occupies the end of the point. It's a community of several hundred shipping containers. The contos, as residential containers are known, form a steel hedge maze. A canopy of pipes and wires sprouts from the metal boxes, shuttling sewage, water, and power. Satellite dishes and solar panels stand in for foliage. Tiny lenses glitter on every surface like chorus-line rhinestones.

Sam secures his motorcycle. Across the road, under the watchful eyes of a blue suede dachshund, his neighbor kneels, hacking at the broken asphalt with a spade. "Morning, Jacob," Sam calls out as he approaches. "How's the garden coming?"

The little mechanical dog starts barking furiously.

Jacob Gaur doesn't look up. "Not so well." Thin as a stick insect, he's a hanger for his logo-freckled sponsor wear. "Quiet, Duke." He stabs his spade into the ground and stands like a marionette whose strings have been yanked. Duke scurries backward to keep from being trodden on.

"Does Duke's bark sound distorted to you?" Jacob asks.

"A bit."

"I'm going to see Tony for a diagnostic later."

Sam looks about warily. "Inside?"

Jacob nods and leads the way into his container.

It's a sty. Bare bulbs dangle over a bird's nest of wires, circuit boards, and salvaged electronics. A plaid sofa bleeding stuffing looks as if it might have summered in the street for a few years before retiring to a quieter life indoors. Beyond is the kitchen and beyond that, the bedroom, each in a more desperate state of disarray. The walls are decorated with free art subsidized by the manufacturers of products depicted.

Sam removes Dr. Mako's glasses from his pocket. "What do you make of these?"

"Nice." Jacob squints, examining the temples. "Old—late nineteenth or early twentieth century, I'd guess."

"See the engraving?"

"J.M. The maker's initials, or maybe the original owner's?"

Sam chuckles. "Why are you asking me?"

"Have you tried to match them on the net?"

"No. I thought I'd ask you first. I rarely get reliable query results when dealing with anything before the turn of the last millennium."

"Yeah, every time those databases change hands, someone

mucks things up in the name of adding value. These are worth a lot, by the way."

"Like how much?"

"A half million maybe."

Sam snorts. "Get out of here."

Jacob points to the copper disks at the ends of the temples. "Because of these."

"They look like electrical contacts."

"I think they are."

"Any idea what they do?"

"A practical joke, maybe?"

"Like a joy buzzer?"

Jacob nods. "Or they could be therapeutic. Doctors did some weird things then."

"Know anyone who might be able to provide more information?"

"No, but if you put them up for auction, someone is bound to recognize them. Set the starting price low, with an unlisted reserve of one billion, so the sale won't process regardless of the bid. You'll end up with a list of antique collectors."

"So when do you get started?"

"You want me to post them?" Jacob beams.

"You've got cred. Buyers know you. When I post, other specs start sniffing around."

"I can do that."

"I'm gonna sleep the rest of the day. Then I'll probably be at Pullman's starting around seven or eight, so I'll be incommunicado. But I'll check in after that."

"Isn't Nadi on the evening shift?"

Sam tries not to catch Jacob's smile. "You fixed for meds?"

Jacob pulls a plastic container from his pocket and rattles it. Drawn by the sound, Duke waddles over and gazes up expectantly.

"One of these days I'm gonna get you an IV implant," Sam says.

Jacob rubs his arm as if he's trying to scrub off his skin. "Don't say that, Sam. You know I hate those things."

"Whatever. Just trying to help."

"I'll let you know when I get some hits."

Algorithmic jazz issues from the jukebox at Pullman's Diner, once a CalTrain car. Sam has complained about the so-called music before, but no one else seems to care. Most people can't tell whether a song came from musicians or mathematics. And with the scrambler on the roof, an audio stream isn't an option.

In the next booth, a scruffy youth branded head to toe with his sponsors' tattoos is haggling over the price of his meal. For the imitation designer watch he's offering in trade, he wants a burger, fries, and dessert.

Nadi holds the watch up as if it's a dead fish. She shakes her head. "A burger, fries, and coffee. That's best I can do."

Over at the counter, a portly man in a business suit is wolfing down a slice of cheesecake. He's probably got the privacy statement on the diner's menu memorized; Sam guesses he comes to Pullman's to keep his caloric indiscretion from fattening his insurance premium. Even at offline dives, there's some risk of surveillance, but tattling opportunists are at least far less efficient than the company bots that query credit-card transactions.

Sam shifts about on the vinyl bench and waves at Nadi. He turns his attention back to his tablet. Dr. Xian Mako stares back at him from the flex-screen.

Reviewing the results of his search, he finds that the dead man has virtually no public history and mentions of him in pay-per-view databases are suspiciously slight: birth records; medical admissions for childhood ailments; some juvenilia from old network archives, consisting mostly of amateur digital imaging. There's a mention in the Lowell High School web archives about his winning the Pharmalis science prize in 2022. A few journal articles following that. Ten years later, there's a video of him receiving his PhD in electroneurology from UC Berkeley. After that, except for a photo of Mako at a Tokyo medical prosthetics conference in 2035 and a donation to the Animal Legal Fund, there's nothing. No one reaches his fifties leaving so few footprints.

Sam leans forward, laying his head on his tablet as if it's a pillow. He stares into the blur of pixels. "You're not going to make this easy, are you, Dr. Mako?" The screen fogs with his breath.

"Long day?"

Looking up, Sam sees Nadi dangling a grease-stained bill. She has seductively crooked teeth, full lips, and a face that reminds him of melancholy Persian cat. Her walk is stiff, like someone who grew up with a back brace; they're still in use abroad. He saw her once in an Indian action film. It was a nonspeaking part. He has never mentioned it to her; he's waiting for the right time.

Far above, fan blades drum the dusk.

"Not really. Been asleep for most of it. Thought I'd get up to see you and the sunset." Sam reaches for the bill and fumbles in his jacket for a pack of cigarettes. He props the plastic packet on the table.

Smiling slightly, Nadi eyes the "Banned in the USA!" sticker on the label. "These are worth a lot, you know."

"How about you credit me the balance?"

"We don't keep those kinds of records, Sammy."

Sam points to his head. "Keep one for me up here."

Nadi pockets the cigarettes. "You're a bad man."

"I love the way that sounds with your accent," Sam says, grinning.

"I hate my accent."

"Why?"

"I just want to fit in, you know?"

Over at the kitchen window, the cook swats the call bell. "I'll remember you for a week, Sammy." Nadi leaves to answer her summons.

The moment Sam steps outside, notification sounds chirp from his tablet and watch. "Christ." He bats at his electronics as if beset by bees.

A Network Services rep replaces Dr. Mako's face on the flex-screen. The contrite expression on her doe-eyed face looks like botched plastic surgery.

"At 8:02 p.m. this evening, a high-energy radio frequency burst interrupted network processes in your neighborhood. I have been trying to alert you for fourteen minutes. Full service will be restored shortly."

Sam barks into the mic on his tablet. "Marilyn, contact Jacob Gaur using any available protocol. Tell him—"

"I'm sorry, Sam," says Marilyn, "but there are no active public streams going into Maerskton. Network Services reports that a high-energy radio frequency burst has interrupted all processes across the publicly accessible spectrum. Do you wish to modify your command?"

"Scan for shielded nodes in the area."

"Do you mean the Maerskton area or your current location?"

"Maerskton."

"Your voice has been recognized. I'm waiting for a capacity check from a San Francisco police dispatch node."

A pause. Sam squeezes through the cluster of cars surrounding the diner; they're parked in any available space—including up on the curb—for lack of legal parking areas. "Come on."

"There are three police cruisers capable of transmission in your neighborhood."

"Authorize packet relay to any available node in Jacob Gaur's residence. Accept all charges."

"Unable to comply. Devices registered to Jacob Gaur are unresponsive."

"Damnit!"

"Please be more specific."

Sam glares at his tablet. "Done. I'm done."

"If you're having trouble with your network connection, why not consider a BigBad Server?"

Sam finally reaches his bike.

"BigBad is the only original equipment manufacturer that uses military-grade shielding and redundant quantum processors for—"

He slides his tablet into his bike's rear pannier, muffling Marilyn's pitch, and rams his helmet onto his head. The engine rumbles to life.

With a twist of the wrist, he roars homeward.

Two police cruisers idle in the street. Their inboard rotors have left the wall of Sam's container pockmarked by scattered gravel. Red laser wards cordon off Jacob's conto. Within the beams, Captain Nial Fox and three of his crew are sweeping the area with full-spectrum lights while waiting for the forensic techs. Just outside the heavy metal door of Jacob's container, Duke stands motionless.

Sam rushes through the warding beams, tripping the siren.

The nearest officer menaces Sam with his stun baton.

Holding up his arms, Sam says, "Jacob Gaur was my friend."

Nial strides over, hands in the pockets of his overcoat. "It's okay. I know him."

The other officer withdraws.

Nodding in gratitude, Sam takes another step toward the container. Nial blocks his way. Sam's fingers curl into a ball, instinctively as a pill bug.

Nial stands his ground. He's a tall man, slightly stooped.

He seems somehow liquid, always moving—a side effect of a reflex implant. His thin lips bend downward as if he's trying to conceal a slice of lemon in his mouth.

"You're not going to let me in?"

Nial shakes his head. "Don't try to hit me again. You're not fast enough anymore."

Looking for a way out of the moment, Sam clenches his jaw.

"Why don't we sit down over there," Nial suggests, placing his hand on Sam's shoulder to guide him.

Sam yanks himself away. "Just tell me if he's dead."

"Quite."

Eyes unblinking, Sam sinks to the pavement.

"I'm sorry, Sam," Nial says, crouching down. His long coat billows about his ankles. "The network doesn't list any emergency contacts. Is there anyone we should inform?"

"No." Sam's voice barely rises above the level of the wind.

The two men remain motionless for several minutes.

Just down the street, half a dozen local residents have gathered, their faces furrowed with worry and anger. Uniforms mean occupation here. Just in case the locals get uppity, one of Nial's crew readies his microwave gun—known unofficially as "a heater" because it makes targets feel like they're burning without doing any lasting harm.

An officer approaches. Nial stands, straightens his coat, and withdraws.

Sam stares blankly at the road beneath him. Every breath bears the weight of someone sitting on his chest. He can't help but think that the glasses got Jacob killed.

A few minutes later, Nial returns. "Jacob's t-file designates you as his executor," he says. "Not that you'll have much to do. He didn't have more than five grand to his name."

"Interested in helping me out?"

Nial shakes his head.

Sam glowers.

"It's not just that there's no money in it, Sam."

"What, you're still angry about that night at Jimmy D's?"

"You're the one who's angry, Sam."

"Spare me the psychoanalysis."

"I don't need another of your goddamn crusades, and I don't need more teeth knocked out." Nial starts back toward his cruiser.

When Nial is halfway across the street, Sam calls out, "Nial, did you find any glasses?"

"No."

"You're sure?"

"What do they look like?"

"Antique. With rose-colored lenses."

"Like I said, we didn't find any. But I'll allow you to look around after the techs have finished their sweep."

Shielding his eyes, Sam watches Nial's cruiser lift off. It won't be long before the techs arrive, but he decides not to wait. The glasses are long gone. He slips across the street to his steel home, to wrestle with his conscience and a bottle of vodka. He looks around for something to hit.

CHAPTER TWO

BY SIX IN the morning, the implant on Sam's wrist displays a blood-alcohol level low enough that he'll be able to enable the ignition chip on his bike. He stumbles into the shower, but the water is off again. Retribution by City Water, no doubt, for buying the basic service package without the pipe-security upgrade. He grabs a bottle of icy water from the fridge to rinse his face.

Taking a seat at his desk, he tries a few more searches, adding terms gleaned during his last attempt, like "Pharmalis" and "electrophysiology." Again, he gets next to nothing. He ups his bid to five hundred on acceptance. The results are the same.

He guesses he's been outbid. Either someone bought his search terms and offered no results—the standard censorship mechanism since editorial and advertising became indistinguishable—or someone is paying specifically to target him with an empty list.

Time to make some offline inquiries.

Marilyn's face appears on the wall-mounted monitor as Sam grabs his leather jacket. "Shall I keep inquiring, Sam?"

"No." Sam pats his pockets. Empty.

"Are you going out?"

"Yes." From a banker's box full of cords and tools, he takes a wall-eye and a radiomark sprayer that resembles a pen.

"Where?"

"Somewhere."

"Please be more specific."

"Why?" Sam asks in a reflexive attempt to shame her.

"So I can arrange for appropriate advertising that will prepare you to enjoy your destination."

Her wounded tone makes Sam shiver. "Marilyn, silence."

"How many minutes would you like to buy?"

"One hundred twenty."

"Transaction processed. I'll catch up with you in two hours, Sam."

"Marilyn, copy local data to my private directory at GeoSync Five. Authorize by voice. Execute local wipe."

He leaves before Marilyn can reply, ashamed of being provoked by software. He doesn't want to be that person again, the one who loses control.

Weaving through surprisingly light traffic on Sixteenth Street with his engine rumbling, Sam fails to hear the street dusters passing overhead. Just as he crosses Mission Street, scented spray soap blankets the road. It's the city's latest scheme to deal with what it calls "indigent persons"—though most people just refer to them as 'gents in mocking reference to the gentlemen they're presumed not to be.

The concoction covering him is a chemical marvel. Its nontoxic microbial scrubbers confer the sort of clean usually only seen on TV; under pressure, the slippery mist turns to sand, aiding tire traction on streets until the next rainfall sends it to the nearest storm drain. As for the fashion-magazine aroma, that's supposed to be a feature rather than a bug—at least for the cosmetics companies getting greater exposure for their celebrity fragrances.

Sam curses himself for going offline and missing the strafing alert. While he doubts Marilyn can take any real joy in his comeuppance, he nonetheless imagines her smiling smugly.

He soon arrives at the Duboce Stalls, a farmer's market without farmers, but full of buyers, sellers, and curiosity-seekers who gather every morning in one of the city's few remaining historic parking lots—all of which are under the protection of the National Parking Service. Conveniently for Sam, scofflaws are out in force, barbecuing with charcoal that masks his scent with smoke.

On a hill behind the market stands the Old Mint, now a day trip for history students and tourists too shortsighted to make reservations at Entertainment Corp's Alcatraz. Off to the west, across the hillside of Twin Peaks, glass windows turn gold under the gaze of the rising sun.

Sam elbows his way to the back of the market, where the antique dealers have set up their booths. Like a Buddha made of gingerbread dough, Amir Urutu sits at his table, arranging the day's featured goods: netsuke figurines, genetically enhanced herbs, and assorted twentieth-century antiques. He nods as Sam approaches.

"Hello, my friend."

"How's business, Amir?"

Amir beams. "Splendid. Have you seen these?" He holds up a pair of black plastic sunglasses. "Auglites. Just got a shipment from China, and they're almost gone."

"What do they do?"

"Dynamic resurfacing."

"You mean overlays?"

"Not simple overlays. These are much better than an eyepiece. They can track your head movements perfectly, no ghosting. These are gonna be big."

Sam glances about. "Got time to chat?"

"Of course. How's your little one doing? I've been meaning to stop by to see her, but you know how it is."

"She still can't see or talk. Her medical rep wants to get her into a drug trial for something called Lucidan. It's supposed to stimulate her brain."

"I hope it works," Amir says, pursing his lips. "I really do."

"Me too." Sam makes an effort to smile. "Speaking of glasses, what do you know about antique specs?"

"Some. What do you want to know?"

"I came across a peculiar pair—rose-colored lenses, zinc wire with a copper disk at the end of each temple, and the letters J.M. engraved on them."

Amir's face lights up. "May I see them?" he asks.

"I don't have them anymore."

"Oh, Sam. Don't tell me you sold them."

"No." Sam doesn't want to reveal too much. "Why? Are they valuable?"

Amir buries his head in his hands. "Yes, very." He reaches beneath the table, produces a tablet, and says, "Sumi, search the Hague patent database for the term 'galvanic spectacles.' Limit results to entries that match the following criteria: Inventor's first name begins with the letter 'J.' Also, inventor's surname begins with the letter 'M.'"

Sumi replies, "One result found."

An illustration of a pair of glasses appears on the flex-screen, bearing the legend "U.S. Patent No. 78534, June 2, 1868, Judah Moses, Hartford CT."

Sam leans over and turns the screen so he can read it more easily.

"My invention consists in the combination, with the temples or front of a pair of spectacles, of an electrogalvanic battery or batteries arranged in such relation that an electrical current may be produced, whereby a person is enabled to apply electricity to the nerves of the head and obtain the therapeutic effects thereof."

So Jacob was right. "I can't imagine they were very effective," Sam observes.

Amir shrugs. "For people who believed in them, they probably worked better than being bled."

"I owe you one. Would you forward the file to me?"

"Of course. You should talk to Kenneth Wren. He's a

dealer, high-end, got a shop on Pacific. If he didn't sell them, he'll know who did."

Sam manages a slight grin and clasps Amir on the shoulder. "Thanks."

"May I ask where you found such glasses?"

"On a dead man. And I lost them on another."

Without further explanation, Sam waves and makes his way back through the crowd.

Standing on Twenty-Sixth Street, a block west of Potrero Avenue, Sam rings the bell at The Sambar Hospice. Peppered with the husks of insects, the light above the door hisses—a dirge for the flies that died within.

After turning several bolts, Maria Sambar admits Sam and opens her arms for an obligatory but kind-hearted hug. She stands at the level of Sam's shoulder, dressed in a skirt and a sleeveless blouse. She wears her dark hair long to hide a disfiguring scar from an acid splash. Her Rubenesque figure suggests that she ignores the diet recommended by her health-insurance company.

Sam wonders how she manages to remain so cheerful with such hopeless patients, but he never dares ask, for fear his pessimism might be catching. Maria's relentless warmth sustains him more than he likes to admit.

"Any change?" Sam removes his leather jacket.

Yawning, Maria shakes her head. "But…"

Sam's eyes widen. "You heard from the rep?"

"Hannah pinged me last night. You must have friends in

high places because Fiona's been accepted in the trial. A transport team from Zvista will be by this afternoon."

Sam punches the air and smiles ear to ear. "Fantastic!"

"I hope it works," says Maria. "Give her the good news."

Sam walks across the worn floorboards of the foyer and passes through the door to his right. In the living room, they're barely alive. Six salvaged hospital beds stand on steel haunches, each at varying degrees of inclination. The still children occupying them seem to be held together by the variety of colorful fabric patches that transmit diagnostic data to display panels at the foot of each bed. Instead of the intravenous lines and clunky machinery found in budget-strapped trauma centers, smart pills, skin pins, and programmable shunts manage the delivery of fluids and medication.

He approaches Fiona and takes a seat by her bed. "Hi honey," he says, leaning forward to brush away the wisps of hair that hang over her closed eyes. He takes her hand in his. "Hannah has managed to get you into a trial for a drug called Lucidan. It's supposed to bring you out of your coma eventually. Some technicians will come by later today to transport you to the research center." He pauses, offering her a chance to respond, then continues. "I won't be here when they come for you, but I'll stop by after you get settled in. Let's keep our fingers crossed, okay?" Gently, he slides her middle finger over her index finger, then lays her hand down.

For half an hour, he talks to his five-year-old daughter—and perhaps she listens. He tells her about his day, without mentioning what happened to Jacob. He describes the sights and sounds and smells as best he can, hoping some detail might nudge her back toward consciousness. That's how Lucidan is supposed to work—by firing sensory neurons, it stimulates the brain. The effect is said to be like a particularly vivid dream, but with a greater physiological response.

He lingers a few minutes longer, saying nothing, remembering too much about the wreck that took his wife, his daughter's mind, and his faith that everything turns out all right in the end. Then he leaves, abruptly, still seeing shattered safety glass sparkling in the headlights. Really, it's light splintered by tears.

CHAPTER THREE

KENNETH WREN'S UNUSUAL Antiques opens at 10:00 a.m. It's only 8:15. Sam scolds himself for failing to check the store's hours before driving across town. Standing among the quaint brick shops on Jackson Street, he glances about, trying to figure out how he'll kill the next two hours. Traffic is unusually heavy. In the thin fog above, a relay blimp bristling with antennas floats just above the Transamerica Pyramid.

There's a gentle beep from the tiny speaker on the collar of Sam's jacket. His two hours of silence are up. "Sam?" Marilyn's voice squeaks. "Are you okay? You haven't moved for two minutes."

Mesmerized, Sam keeps staring at the prickly blimp. A bus passes, ghostly in its electric silence.

"Sam? Please answer me."

A few years ago, a Sino-German consortium announced the construction of several hundred lufts—lofts suspended by mammoth Levitas airships—above the coast of Queensland, Australia. But what began as a compromise between anti-immigrant Aussies and politicians courting the island continent's powerful Asian voting block quickly took off, both figuratively and literally. Far from being punitive, luft living afforded seclusion and security unavailable to harried pavement dwellers. And the views were to die for. The few refugees from occupied Taiwan who resettled in the initial luft cluster packed up and sold out when the offers became too good to pass up. After that, the developers went global.

Sam struggles every time he sees the network interstitials depicting an exclusive luft community moored to the cinderblock reef off the Florida Keys. He imagines that life in the air will be somehow less laden with mundane concerns.

"Sam, you haven't eaten in twelve hours. The Old Fog Diner is located just half a mile north of your location. The diner is offering a 15 percent discount for network referral walk-ins. Would you like to hear some customer recommendations?"

Sam glowers. "No, Marilyn, I really wouldn't."

"Maybe your appetite would improve if you went to the gym."

"What's my grid debt?"

"You owe 0.7412 kilowatt hours."

"So where's the nearest Station?"

The Power Station on Broadway and Columbus is busy for a

Tuesday morning. Sam inquires about the crowd while buying some disposable sweats at the front desk.

The attendant, a wiry brunette with the physique of a mannequin, scowls from behind her bulletproof-plastic window. "Apart from a few stock-market jocks, they're mostly addicts trying to meet their community service and baseline health contracts," she answers. "A Probation Nation drive-thru just opened on Clay Street."

"Pretty fit-looking bunch of junkies."

"You should see the guys who shoot Andro."

"I said 'fit,' not 'freakish.'"

Sam follows the sign to the men's dressing room. The scent of perspiration and bleach lingers amid metal lockers. He guesses it'll take him seven hours to generate three-quarters of a kilowatt hour. Back when he fought in the ring, it might have been possible in six, but he's been out of training for too long to sustain that kind of output. Not that it matters. His sweats are only rated to last ninety minutes before disintegrating.

Just after ten, his outfit now stylishly ragged, Sam dismounts from the stationary bicycle and offers a polite goodbye to the anonymous New Yorker he's been racing over the network. He showers, dresses, and hits the street humming the Gut Buster jingle that was hounding him during his ride.

Outside, it's a sunny North Beach morning. Sam threads his way through the tourists. He waves at the security camera at Montgomery and Broadway, figuring his friend Tony Roan might be fielding surveillance hits for the city today. They did some break-in jobs together a number of years ago, before the stability of government contract work weaned Tony from the spec's life.

It occurs to Sam that his former partner might have access to cameras run by the National Park and Mining Service. "Marilyn, finger Tony Roan at the Department of Surveying."

"He's in a meeting."

"Send him a voice message. Begin: Hi Tony. It's Sam Crane. I hope all's well. Listen, I need a favor. I'm working a murder that took place in the headlands about two a.m. on the morning of the second. I was wondering if you could ask around and see if there's any video coverage out there. It'd make my day to see it if so. Ciao. End message."

"Message sent, Sam. Based on speech analysis, the network has determined that your call was business-related. You will be billed accordingly." The tone of Marilyn's voice shifts from informational to evangelical. "If you're ever struggling to find the right words, Electric Expressions can help. With Electric Expressions' patented NewVoice real-time audio sweetening, we take the ums, ahs, and awkward pauses out of your voice mail so you sound smarter. If you act now and send a NewVoice-enhanced message before the end of May, we'll add a moving, contextually appropriate soundtrack to the mix, absolutely free."

Sam tries to drown Marilyn out by humming some more. It's futile, though; the speakers in his collar come equipped with an automatic gain compensator. Even the rumble of a street cleaner wouldn't silence her. He's been tempted to install a volume attenuator in his jacket, but hacking the piezoelectric thread used in network-enabled clothing isn't as easy as rewiring his motorcycle helmet.

Reaching the antique shop, he opens the glass door, finding it heavier than he expects—bulletproof, no doubt. As he steps inside, the pneumatic security gate at the far side of the foyer slides open and the door behind him clicks shut. He guesses the mirror on the wall conceals an identification system.

Kenneth Wren sits upright at an antique desk embellished with gold leaf. He wears a cream-colored suit and a matching turtleneck that presents his slender face as if it were one of the artworks in the room. His small eyes dart between Sam and the monitor that is almost certainly displaying Sam's public file.

"Come in, Mr. Crane."

The Bach playing in the background fades to accommodate conversation. Sam approaches slowly, entranced by the splendid antiques. "Good morning," he says.

"You must pay a lot to have so little in your file. I like that in a man."

"Money or secrets?"

"Is there one without the other?" Kenneth asks.

Sam offers a faint smile in reply. "Sometimes. But I'm afraid I may disappoint you. I have far more secrets than money. I'm a spec."

"Ah, what a pity." Kenneth pouts. "I had so hoped to plumb the depths of your pockets."

"I have a few questions."

"Are you logging?"

"Marilyn, offer privacy. Use Threefish encryption. Accept all charges."

"Attention," Marilyn calls out. "Sam Crane is requesting a private conversation. If you accept, all local sensors, including but not limited to video, audio, molecular, seismic, geospatial, biometric, and thermal monitoring devices, will be disabled until reactivated by voice, except for sensors required under secret law. Mutual consent will be required for reactivation if accepting parties remain within fifty feet. Those present must signal their willingness to participate by stating their names and their dispositions."

Glancing at the monitor on his desk, Kenneth nods. "Kenneth Wren. I accept."

"All logging suspended at 10:36 a.m. by request," answers a voice that sounds vaguely familiar. "Service charges billed to Sam Crane."

"Orson Wells?" Sam asks.

Kenneth grins. "A student of the Golden Age."

"Now there's a name for you. Much better than 'Dylan Michelob.'"

"Or 'Samantha Virgin,'" Kenneth adds with understated contempt. "Though if he'd been offered a naming deal, I imagine he'd have taken it."

"I didn't realize Wells had become available. Always liked the sound of his voice."

"Just last year. His heirs fell on hard times."

Sam sits down. "I've been thinking about retiring Marilyn. She's been getting on my nerves."

"They did a good job with Mr. Wells. He smolders." Wren gestures lazily. "So what brings you here?"

"Are you familiar with galvanic spectacles?"

"Indeed." Kenneth's eyebrows bob. "Lovely medical antiquities."

"Ever sell a pair to a doctor by the name of Xian Mako?"

"I can't discuss client purchases or inquiries, unless you have a warrant."

"Would it be worth my while to get one?"

After pondering the question, Kenneth shakes his head.

"Come on, help me out here. We're off the record."

"Mr. Crane, my clients rely on my discretion."

Folding his arms, Sam makes no effort to conceal his annoyance.

"The man you want to pester is Roderick Pigeon. He runs an antique shop in London specializing in medical devices."

"Will you send me his profile?"

"Orson, forward Roderick Pigeon's public key set to Sam Crane."

"Done," says Orson Wells.

"Thanks for your help."

Before passing through the security gate, Sam turns and leans against the doorframe. "You never asked what I'm looking for."

"That's true."

"Most do."

"Could be I already know."

"That's what I think."

Kenneth waves and faces his desktop monitor.

Sam lingers, jaw clenched.

"Quit while you're ahead, Mr. Crane," Kenneth says without looking up.

Sam returns to where he was sitting. "You're a brave man to talk like that. You must have a high-end personal defense system. A Heliolith Guardian maybe?"

Kenneth hoists an awkward smile as he crosses his arms.

"Yeah, that's a good system," Sam continues. "Tetanizing lasers can be targeted very precisely. But the Heliolith triggering algorithm has some flaws. The personal boundary check doesn't return a fire command unless the motion detector has gone off too. But the motion detector's default threshold is set too high. It only detects very sudden movements."

Casually, Sam reaches across the desk and takes hold of Kenneth's shirt.

"Orson!" Kenneth cries, startled.

"Yes, Kenneth?"

Sam releases his grip and steps back. "If you quit when you're ahead, you never know how far you can go."

Lips curled in contempt, Kenneth brushes away the wrinkles in his shirt.

"Can I be of assistance?" Orson inquires.

"No, never mind." Kenneth glares at Sam. "I could have called the police."

Sam clasps his hands behind his back. "The bill for their visit would be more than my fine. Look, a friend of mine's dead because of those damn glasses. Maybe Dr. Mako too. I can't get a warrant because I'm not police, but I can get a subpoena. And if I have to rummage through your records, it could be very disruptive to your business."

"I don't like being pushed around, Mr. Crane."

"And I don't like having to push you around." Sam doesn't convince either of them.

Kenneth snorts. "With the right drugs, you'd be charming company. Now get out."

With a shrug, Sam leaves.

Across the street, beside an antimicrobial hydrant, stands a bus shelter. Sam walks over to it, palming the wall-eye in his pocket. Casting a furtive glance back over his shoulder, he bends down, plants the dime-sized lens at the base of the shelter, and presses once to activate it. The tiny disc shimmers, adjusting its color to match its surroundings, and then begins its vigil.

In a dingy teleconferencing booth that has been splashed with cheap perfume to mask scents far worse, Sam waits for Roderick Pigeon to appear. A Dupont Whiskey spot plays in 3D over the viewing glass, which is angled like a windshield to redirect and split the ceiling-bound projector beam. The star of the ad, a tough lounging in a smoking jacket, is rendered in real time to resemble Sam. The woman pouring his drink is generated with only a G-string, as per his solicitation preferences. He'd enjoy a full frontal pitch even more, but there are purchasing requirements, and Sam is trying to be thrifty.

Sam wipes the projection lens, but the image quality doesn't improve. From the look of it, someone has scratched the glass. "Marilyn," he asks, "has the Medical Examiner filed anything on Dr. Xian Mako yet?"

"Please be more specific."

Sam rolls his eyes. "Has the Medical Examiner filed a report on Dr. Xian Mako's cause of death?"

"Yes. The report was filed at 9:17 a.m. today."

"What was the cause of death?"

"Tetrodotoxin."

Sam leans forward, pressing against the greasy touch pad used by those unable to speak. "Reference, summary only."

"Tetrodotoxin is a powerful neurotoxin that causes death in approximately 60 percent of humans who ingest it," Marilyn says with a bit too much enthusiasm. "It can be found in the liver, gonads, intestines, and skin of fish in the Tetraodontoidea family, which includes ocean sunfishes, porcupine fishes, and fugu."

"Marilyn, copy reference details to my private directory at GeoSync Five, along with the Medical Examiner's report. Authorize by voice."

"Your request has been received, Sam." Her voice suddenly sultry, Marilyn continues, "If you're interested in exotic seafood, you should really try Aquamarine. It's the only restaurant in Northern California licensed to serve fugu, the blowfish much beloved in Japan. Chef Shingen Saba hasn't lost a customer in fifteen years. His five-course fixed-price menu includes hireshu, sashimi tessa, and tetchiri stew. For those who prefer to be reassured, Aquamarine will run a toxin test on your fugu for an extra $490—and no one will think any less of you. In seven months, on December 3, a table for two will be available at 6:00 p.m. Would you like to make a reservation?"

"No, Marilyn." Sam continues waiting for his call to go through. He recalls the wounds on Dr. Mako's body. If Mako was poisoned, such cuts might have been inflicted post mortem, in anger. The alternative—that he was tortured and then force-fed fugu—makes no sense. The facial mutilation means its personal. He knows the feeling, an adrenaline-drunk rage that's owned him for years. It's an understanding he longs to give up.

"Handshake received," Marilyn finally says. "Begin transmission."

The image of an elderly man with sparse gray hair appears, hovering in the air. Only his torso is visible. "Mr. Crane, what can I do for you?" he inquires.

"Hello. I was referred to you by Kenneth Wren, here in San Francisco. Do you have time to answer a few questions?"

"I was just about to head home for the day."

"Let's make this brief, then. I'm looking into the death of Dr. Xian Mako. A pair of galvanic spectacles was found on his body. I think whoever killed him left the glasses on his corpse deliberately. I'd like to know why."

Roderick's eyes widen. "Dr. Mako is dead?"

"Yes. I take it you knew him?"

"I wouldn't say that. He was a frequent customer of mine. We exchanged a few messages, but that was the extent of our correspondence. It's dreadful to think that he was murdered."

"Frequent? He had a thing for antiques?"

"He preferred owning products outright rather than licensing them. A lot of Americans shop here for that reason."

"Do you recall selling him a pair of galvanic spectacles?"

"Oh, yes." Roderick purses his lips. "Those particular glasses were made by Judah Moses, who received a patent for them. Quite an interesting fellow, if you care for such things."

"Did they have any special significance?"

"Supposedly, they heightened the wearer's sight by applying electric current to the optic nerve. They're highly sought after by collectors of medical quackery."

Sam nods. "Makes sense, with Mako being a doctor and all."

"Actually, I believe he bought them as a gift."

"Is that what he said?"

"Not exactly. But he did ask to have them gift wrapped."

"Any idea who he intended to give them to?"

Roderick shakes his head. "I'm afraid not."

"Is there anything you can tell me about him? Like who he worked for?"

"As I said, I really didn't know the man."

Sam pauses. "Well, thank you. I appreciate your help."

With a wave, Roderick logs off.

Sam steps out of the booth, relieved to escape the celebrity-scent knockoff. "Marilyn, find a registered health insurance company outside the country that's willing to carry an anonymous search of the Medical Information Bureau's medical records database for under one thousand dollars. Find claims made by Dr. Xian Mako or his dependents, if any.

Copy results to a transient cache, establish an encrypted connection, then summarize and delete."

Marilyn replies with another pitch, but her words go unheard.

Standing on the street corner, Sam revisits his encounter with Kenneth Wren. Something doesn't fit. Wren wouldn't talk about his own customers, but he pointed him to the Englishman. Assuming the two dealers have mutual clients, the prudent thing to do would be to say nothing at all. Maybe Wren's concern is protecting himself rather than his customers? Has he been threatened?

Marilyn becomes more insistent. "Sam, would you like to receive a quote?"

"I'm sorry, Marilyn. A quote for what?"

"A quote for data insurance."

"Some other time."

"Please be more specific."

"May 3, 2150," Sam says. He tries not to sound spiteful; he doesn't want to trigger one of her pouting loops.

"Your datebook only goes to 2143."

"Can't you extend it?"

"The one-hundred-twenty-eight-year limit is generous, considering the current average human life span."

"Who knows? I might live to one hundred and thirty."

"That's statistically unlikely. Your current estimated date of death is 2089."

"At seventy-four? It was 2091 a few months ago!"

"Your intake of saturated fat has been exceeding recommended levels since last July."

"Has my health insurance premium gone up?"

"Yes, by 2 percent."

Sam mutters sarcastically, "Gee, I wonder if that's why I got a pitch from Aquamarine."

Marilyn offers helpfully, "Your recommendation from Aquamarine was based on the following factors: topic match, tetrodotoxin, 53 percent; skipped meal flag, breakfast, 12 percent..."

Sam is reminded that he is hungry and begins to think about lunch.

Marilyn drones on. "...dining history type match, seafood, 11 percent; dietary noncompliance flag, 9 percent..."

Sam gives Marilyn and the network the finger—a gesture that would appear to passersby to be directed at the heavens.

"...search history association match, Dr. Xian Mako, 8 percent; establishment rating, excellent, 7 percent."

"Dr. Mako?" Sam laughs aloud. It hadn't occurred to him that Aquamarine might have been the source of the poison that killed Dr. Mako. But of course it has to have been. It's the only restaurant licensed to serve fugu in Northern California. "Marilyn, I could kiss you."

"If you're looking for female companionship," she suggests, "why not call the Vivid Doll House? Vivid's auto-mates feature secreting orifices and pseudoskin on a lightweight bone frame for a feeling that's real. And with Vivid's new Network Services interface, you can talk to your girl like you're talking to me, starting at only $215 an hour. Haven't you ever wondered what it would feel like to hold me, Sam?"

"No, Marilyn." It's easier to lie.

Astride his Ducati, Sam takes Geary Street across to Japantown. The red lights along the way display a promiscuity promo. Sponsored by the Chinese-backed Church of Christ Capitalist, the campaign aims to counter the falling birth rate among California's affluent Chinese expats, a demographic trend that's cutting into the Church's overseas tithing take. Though its audio track is broadcast in Mandarin, the steamy spot's crossover appeal has been snarling traffic as drivers linger through several light changes for encore presentations.

Outside Aquamarine, a lone environmental protester wearing a sandwich-board display dodges back and forth, vying for attention with five paid counter-protesters. The "contesters" match his movements, hoping the malcontent's message will get lost amid their own sandwich-board displays. A glimpse of the video screen worn by the protester reveals a commercial trawler cutting through an ocean dark with blood. But as the contesters close around him again, all that Sam sees are ads extolling the health benefits of seafood.

A valet in a Mao jacket approaches and steadies Sam's motorcycle while Sam dismounts, giving a reverent nod as he takes the classic bike under his protection.

Behind the glass doors, the meticulously attired staff is preparing for the lunch rush. Men and women in business dress line the bar, waiting for the 11:30 a.m. seating. The live fish in the display tanks appear less animated, as if aware of their inevitable relocation to someone's plate.

Sam asks the maitre d' where he can find the manager,

Tetsuo Washi. He's directed to the mezzanine lounge at the top of the stairs, just beyond the bar.

On his way up, he passes a sharply dressed man with the beginnings of a dark beard. Ordinarily, Sam wouldn't give such an encounter further thought, but the man's expression as they exchange glances strikes him as oddly smug. He stops and watches him descend, trying to place the face. At the landing, the man looks back over his shoulder, wearing a hint of a grin, and then continues on.

Perplexed, Sam ascends the last few steps, almost colliding with the manager, who's about to head downstairs himself. Recognizing the tall restaurateur from the image he requested on his way over, Sam introduces himself.

Tetsuo nods politely. "A spec? What brings you here?"

"A patron of yours. Dr. Xian Mako. He was found dead yesterday morning with fugu poison in his system."

"That's most unfortunate. Dr. Mako was a good customer."

"Do you have a moment to talk?" Sam gestures at the nearby banquette.

Taking a seat, Tetsuo leans forward. "I assure you that we had nothing to do with his death. Dr. Mako hasn't dined here for several months."

"I understand the delicacy of this matter."

Tetsuo inclines his head in acknowledgement.

Sam continues, "If he was here the night before last, I wouldn't have to mention it in my report to the city. Any number of vendors might be importing blowfish illegally."

"Your discretion is most appreciated, but as I said, Dr. Mako hasn't dined here recently."

Tetsuo's insistence seems genuine enough, but Sam finds it hard to give up on so obvious a link between victim and poison. "Would you do me the favor of allowing me access to your records?"

"You know I cannot do that without a warrant."

"I can get one," Sam bluffs. "But it's something of an inconvenience."

Hands pressed together as if in prayer, propped up by his elbows, Tetsuo weighs Sam's request. "I don't wish to be rude, Mr. Crane. Perhaps you could query our database through my assistant?"

"Works for me."

"Matsushima, Mr. Crane here would like to ask you a few questions about a customer, Xian Mako. Please answer him directly through external speakers using authorized guest permissions."

The gentle voice of a young woman replies, "Yes, sir. Proceed, Mr. Crane."

"Matsushima, when did Dr. Xian Mako last dine here?"

"January 21, 2050."

Just a few months ago. "Did he order fugu?"

"Yes."

"Was he alone?"

"No."

"Who was with him?"

"I'm sorry, Mr. Crane, but you cannot access that information."

Gritting his teeth, Sam struggles to remember which query protocols he can use in limited-access situations. It seems unlikely he'll be able to find out what he wants to know directly, but it might be possible to arrive at the truth though a more circuitous route.

"Matsushima, how much was the bill for Dr. Mako's table that night?"

"Thirty thousand two hundred forty dollars."

Checking the menu, Sam sees that works out nicely to four six-thousand-dollar prix fixe dinners with tax and tip. Considering the cost, Aquamarine's clientele, and the doctor's apparent lack of family, it's likely a business dinner.

"Matsushima, was there any change in Dr. Mako's available credit between 6:00 p.m. on January 21 of this year and 1:00 a.m. the following morning?"

"No, there was no change."

So Mako didn't pay. Sam wonders if the evening was a freebie of some sort, possibly from a would-be employer or business associate. Perhaps it was an act of solidarity that all four diners risked their lives that night. It would be fitting behavior for an outing meant to foster corporate esprit de corps. Certainly the lack of a toxin-scan charge suggests some measure of fraternal bravado among the diners. Or a desire not to offend the chef.

"This is all very interesting, Mr. Crane," Tetsuo says, "but what does it have to do with what happened yesterday or the day before?"

"Probably nothing," Sam admits as he stands. One more question comes to mind. "By the way, do you know who was working Mako's table that evening?"

Tetsuo drums his fingers together. "I'd prefer it if you didn't bother my staff, Mr. Crane."

"Whatever. Thank you for your help."

Descending the stairs, Sam nearly succumbs to the scent of steamed salmon and ginger. Despite his hunger, he keeps walking toward the door.

CHAPTER FOUR

THE GAS SALOON on Divisadero reeks of exhaust. Patrons of the converted body shop like it that way. There are no tables; the car collectors prefer parking inside, where they and their precious machines can see and be seen. The idling of engines precludes the possibility of music, but no one seems to mind—the effect perhaps of a carbon-monoxide buzz.

Sam pulls up to the bar, an auto lift raised waist-high. Beside him, a biker sporting a Confederate kepi is buffing his Harley. The bartender, a lanky Irishman named Sean, looks up.

"What'll you have, Sam?"

"What are you sampling?"

"Got a fine 1997 from here in California, refined at Tosco, thirty cents an ounce."

"Ninety-two octane?"

Sean nods. "I also have a pungent 1999 from Yukos' Kuibyshev facility, infused with naphthalene mothballs. You'll probably have to clean your valves afterwards, but it burns quite nicely. 'Tisn't cheap, though."

"Any racing fuel?"

"I have about a gallon of propylene oxide. But it's noxious stuff. I can't really recommend it."

"Let me try the '97."

Sean dons rubber gloves. Placing a demitasse on the bar, he stretches a pressurized hose from a stainless-steel keg and pours a splash of fuel.

Sam swirls the liquid to check for sediment, then sniffs. The sharp scent burns his nostrils. "Okay, I'll take two hundred fifty-six ounces."

"J.D., issue two gallons of Tosco '97 to Sam Crane," Sean says to his agent.

"Awaiting approval," the creaky voice of John D. Rockefeller replies.

Marilyn chimes in. "Sam, will you accept a debit from the Gas Saloon?"

"Yes, Marilyn."

The light on the fuel keg goes from red to green. Sam takes the hose from Sean and fills up his fuel tank. To him, it's an intimate act, feeding his machine. More modern devices are far more emotionally assertive, with their simulated intelligence and their plaintive manipulation. But compared to the primal act of refueling, such artifice leaves him cold.

Toward the far wall, a restored 1979 Ford Pinto painted

with flames stands with its hood yawning wide. Three paunchy men lean into the car's maw, entranced by the engine.

After scanning the familiar menu, Sam settles for Jelly Chicken, Like Fries, and pirate cola—which tastes every bit as real as the real thing, despite assertions to the contrary by Global Cola. Unfortunately, the same can't be said for vat patties; free-range meat has far more flavor than the stuff grown in test tubes. The $300-per-pound price tag makes it even harder to swallow.

Slipping on his earbud and eye tap, Sam checks his messages while he eats. There's a voice file from Tony Roan: "Hi, Sam. Tony here. The video you asked about doesn't exist. It seems the cameras were removed from the headlands at the beginning of year, as a result of result of a lawsuit filed three years ago by the Modesty Foundation, one of those morality PACs. Apparently, some National Parking Service employee was streaming the feed, which included explicit scenes of animals mating. It gets better: The Tissue Growers of America filed an amicus brief alleging that video of live animals harms its members financially by making live animals more appealing than lab flesh. So no pictures. I hear the FBI may still have some fixed lenses in the area, but they're almost never in working order, thanks to the eco-thugs. Most of the agencies are using drones now because of that. Anyway, I hope that helps. This is making me miss the old days. Let's get together for a beer soon. Ciao."

Sam resists the urge to bury his head in his hands, not wanting to drive his eye tap into his head.

A message from Luis offers no solace. It's the official crime scene report. As expected, genetic material from over five thousand men and women was found on or near the body. Some two thousand of those individuals have criminal records.

Another message proves more promising. A Dutch insurance company accepted his offer to search the Medical Information Bureau's database. Contained in the forwarded report is Dr. Mako's home address.

Yanking his eye tap off, Sam shakes his head in an effort to reestablish reality. But despite his disorientation, he's grinning. Next stop: Green Street.

By the time Luis arrives at Dr. Mako's flat, Sam is scowling, having been there for forty-five minutes already. The well-dressed policeman climbs the steps with the assistance of his umbrella, marking his approach with the clack of metal on concrete. A particularly tall officer follows behind him.

"Sorry I'm late." Luis pats his hair flat, though gale-force winds would be impotent against his pomade. "Had to break up a fight between a couple of 'gents in the Tenderloin."

Sam stows his tablet and hefts a flimsy smile. He's familiar with "disencampment incentives," the bureaucratic term for beating loiterers. "No problem," he says. "Been running around like a madman all morning. I was just catching up on the news."

"Anything interesting?"

"The war for eyeballs continues. A bunch of Content Corp billboards were hacked last night. Entertainment Corp denies responsibility, and meanwhile is accusing Content Corp of polluting its ad stream with blank vector files. Seems not one of the fill areas sold in Casablanca last night had the sponsor's logo."

Luis shrugs. "They sabotage each other to get free coverage."

"There was some outbreak in Brazil. But it was in the pay-per-view section."

"Ignorance costs more."

Sam exhales slowly, trying to come up with a response that doesn't involve his fist and Luis' jaw. Silence is the best he can do.

"You know Karl Midge?"

Rising from his seat on the stoop, Sam offers his hand. "Sam Crane."

"Karl," says the towering policeman, as if rationing his words. Without further ceremony, he kneels before the door and sets to work on the lock.

Luis leans on his umbrella. "This is unlike you, playing things by the book."

"This isn't the sort of case I usually take on," Sam answers. "If I'd known you were gonna be so late, I'd have kicked the door in to spare myself the grief."

"I'm just giving you a hard time."

"You've given me nothing," Sam snaps. "Mako's been dead for over thirty-six hours. It's taken me this long just to figure out where he lived!"

"I'm here, aren't I?"

"Like I said, I should've just kicked in the damn door."

"Quit whining. You knew this wouldn't be a quick close."

"I didn't know Jacob would get killed."

Luis nods sympathetically. "I saw the report. I'm really sorry."

Sam considers telling Luis he doesn't blame him. But he can't.

Karl rises from his knees, expressionless, and opens the door.

A central hallway runs the length of the flat, terminating in a living room with a view of the bay. A scent that's somewhere between ammonia and yeast lingers in the air—someone must have cleaned.

Sam notices the pristine maple floor as he steps inside. No polymers here. It's real wood, $500 dollars a square foot at least, and installed recently. Stunning ukiyo-e prints adorn the walls. If Dr. Mako was unemployed, it was because he didn't need to work.

The three men search the apartment. The job goes quickly because there are no personal effects to be found. No family pictures. No trash. The food in the refrigerator consists of unopened, recently purchased packages.

Finally, Sam says, "There's nothing here. It's like a show home."

Casting a glance at Karl, who's busy taking air-trace samples with a mass spectrometer, Luis nods. "What do you want me to do about it?"

"I don't know. But I've never seen you so disinterested in a case."

"I got a lot on my plate, Sam."

"I should cut my loses and file my report right now."

Luis bristles. "After two days? You know that'll get me audited."

"It'd serve you right for throwing me into the deep end."

"Man, you sure can whine."

"Don't put this off on me. This kind of case should be handled at an official level, not dumped like some low-priority mugging. In fact, I'm surprised the Feds aren't all over this, much less you and yours."

From down the hallway, Karl chimes in, "That smell is BioClean, by the way."

Furrows crease Luis' brow.

"BioClean?" Sam asks.

"Engineered microbes. They eat hair and dead skin, produce ammonia, and die. It's the luxury alternative to genetic decoys."

"So much for DNA evidence. How difficult is it to obtain the stuff?"

"Very, unless you work in the intelligence community."

"You want to tell me what's going on here, Luis?"

"Karl, excuse us for a moment." Luis leads the way into the bedroom and shuts the door.

Splintered daylight breaks through the blinds. In an aquarium beneath the window, fake tropical fish—red scats and striped monos—execute their programs to the soothing sound of the tank's otherwise-pointless air pump.

Addressing his agent, Luis asks for privacy.

Sam accepts and leans back against the door, arms folded.

"You gotta let this one go, Sam."

"Why?"

"I know you'd do anything for your kid," Luis says, his voice taut. "It's the same for me."

After a moment, Sam understands. "Did someone threaten your boy?"

"I can't talk about it, even offline."

"I can't help if you don't tell me what this is about."

"I don't want your help. I want this case buried."

"Well, Jacob's being buried tomorrow. Let's entomb the records with his casket and forget all about it." Not that Jacob left enough for anything other than a biodegradable urn; even Luis probably couldn't save up enough to be buried when he died.

Luis meets Sam's sarcasm with a cold stare. "Give it a month, file your report, and forget all about Dr. Mako. Take the fall. Please."

Grabbing Luis by his coat, Sam shoves him against the wall. "You gave this case to me because you thought the Solve-O-Matic was more likely than I was to come up with a perp!"

Sam takes Luis' silence as confirmation. He releases the policeman and turns toward the bedroom window. Beyond the rooftops, he can see the Golden Gate Bridge straddling a stream of cargo ships stacked with containers, their comings and goings choreographed from Angel Island by sea traffic control. In the sky beyond, planes queue for the automated decent into San Francisco International. At a lower altitude, air trucks and corporate sky cars zigzag along the narrow flight paths required by neighborhood noise ordinances.

But the clockwork world is a bourgeois mirage. The law of the land—in practice, the law of the network—bends for the rich, breaks for the criminal, and betrays the poor. Sam knows better than to expect justice by default. But America markets itself so well that consumers of the dream keep coming, never mind the defective merchandise. The ad always exceeds the experience.

"Take care of yourself, Luis," Sam mutters. "Your kid too." He makes a point of not slamming the door on his way out.

A mediocre rendition of "Honeysuckle Rose" drifts from the maw of the Twenty-Fourth Street BART subway station and up the still escalator. There's a busker below feigning a trumpet solo to prerecorded music. Pirate live concerts do occur, and are usually better than Entertainment Corp's canned versions. But the city's gunshot-location system—not coincidentally, funded by Entertainment Corp—can identify unlicensed performances and dispatch copyright enforcement agents in minutes.

The sounds go unnoticed by the teens wearing counter-camera face paint who glide by on gyro-stabilized scooters. They're deaf to insurrection, preferring instead songs about rebellion from artists who exist only in the minds of marketing execs.

It would be enough to make Sam sick if the homeless hadn't beaten him to it. 'Gents redolent of wine and urine lie sprawled on the sidewalk beside overstuffed shopping carts.

The more ambitious among them gather garbage they'll spin into gold. Recycling earns some a skimpy income, but the real money comes from hoarding. Or more precisely, from extortion. The city pays the Homeless Union well to keep the 'gents from dumping their trash en masse.

Sam loiters with the winos, leaning on his motorcycle. He's keeping an eye on The Third Eye, a psychic supply store that has spared no expense on neon signage. The apartment above is home to Ernesto Cebra, the waiter who served Mako's table four months earlier. A call to Aquamarine under false pretenses was enough to learn the man's name. Sam doubts now that Tetsuo's earlier protectiveness of his staff was anything more sinister than reflex.

Ernesto emerges about fifteen minutes later, short, serious-looking. He wears a pressed white shirt and black pants, newly shined shoes, and a black jacket.

The moment Sam calls his name, Ernesto turns and runs.

Sam takes off in pursuit. Mission Street blurs. A woman emerges from a doorway. A glancing blow. Sam careens into an ice-cream pushcart, stumbles, and keeps going. Spanish curses follow.

Ernesto crosses Twenty-Fifth Street as the light is turning. The waiting cars accelerate. Sam does too. A screech and a horn to his right. He leaps up, rolls onto the hood, and tumbles to the asphalt beside the curb.

Struggling for the breath hammered from his lungs, Sam hauls himself to his feet. His left hand looks like he's been massaging a cheese grater.

The car stops. The driver gets out and starts shouting something about the hood. Bystanders watch, accustomed to seeing conflict as entertainment.

Ernesto is halfway down the block.

The shouting draws nearer. Sam turns. A big man with a beer belly points in accusation. "You scratched the goddamn plastic!" He shoves Sam.

Sam decks him with a practiced right to the gut. He stands seething over the crumpled man, exultant. Too much so. His exhilaration sickens him.

Horns sound.

The man staggers back to his car, eyes pinched with hate. "You'll be sorry," he growls.

Sam watches the man drive away, more disappointed in himself than sorry. Then he's distracted by a commotion up the block. A small crowd has gathered where he last saw Ernesto.

A police cruiser thunders over the rooftops. It must've been on patrol nearby. Sam resigns himself to a night in jail. He should know better. But the cruiser passes by, descending further up the street. He follows, burying his bloody left hand in a wad of tissue in his pocket.

The vehicle's downdraft disperses the onlookers. Ernesto remains, hands bound with plastic ties. He's being questioned by two uniformed officers from the cruiser and a hooker—presumably an undercover cop he had the bad luck to run into.

Sam introduces himself and explains his interest in Ernesto. At the mention of Luis's name, the cops relax, as if among one of their own.

"What'd you do to light a fire under this guy?" the undercover cop asks, adjusting her bustier.

"He just bolted."

"I thought you were someone else," Ernesto says.

One of the officers rolls his eyes. "You want to explain?"

"I haven't done anything wrong."

"You were speeding."

"Come on, man. Speeding?"

"Misdemeanor, Vehicle Code Section 4000.15."

"Reckless ambulation," the second elaborates. "Good for a sleepover downtown."

"And a fine," the first officer adds.

Ernesto looks up in despair. There's no help forthcoming from above. "I owe some money, okay?"

Sam says, "You mind if I ask him something?"

"Fire away," says the second officer.

"How you doin', Ernesto?"

The diminutive waiter snorts. "How the hell do you think?"

"Look, I'm sorry about this. I'm looking into the death of a guy who used to eat at Aquamarine, Dr. Xian Mako. He dined there back in January. It'd really help me if you could remember something about the people he was with."

"Why should I help you?"

"'Cause maybe if you're helpful, our friends here won't arrest you." Sam glances at the cops, guessing they'd rather not deal with the arrest forms, and is rewarded with reluctant nods of agreement.

A bit more at ease, Ernesto scratches his ear with his shoulder. "January was a long time ago. I serve a lot of tables."

"Dr. Mako ordered fugu. There were three others with him. The bill was $25,600."

Ernesto nods. "Okay, I do remember that. Some sort of party."

"Names?"

"Sorry. But they charged the meal to a company called Biopt."

Suppressing a grin, Sam asks Ernesto to spell it out.

"Is that all?"

"One more thing. Did Dr. Mako come in on Sunday?"

"Not that I know of."

Sam nods, thinking through permutations of what might have happened. If Mako didn't come to the poison, perhaps the poison came to him. "Who supplies fugu to the restaurant?"

"Ikura Industries. I forget where they are."

"Ikura Industries is on Pier 29," Marilyn volunteers.

"Thanks, Ernesto. I appreciate your help."

Following handshakes with the cops, Sam heads back to his bike. He's thinking about Marilyn. As much as he resents her constant attention, he can't help but feel flattered.

The Zvista Research Hospital stands across from the UCSF Medical Center on Third Street, just south of SlimNow Park. (SlimNow Inc. bought the naming rights to the stadium when company executives recognized the potential synergy between its calorie-control regimen and the stadium's booming concessions business.)

Sam arrives in the parking lot and gets off his bike. He's eager to see how his daughter is taking the change of scene.

Several packages scurry by, coifed with gripping tendrils that resemble spaghetti. Unlike passive containers, glom boxes arrange their own transportation by scuttling between hitched rides, when they're too heavy to be sent by drone. A box clinging to the roof of one's car is usually a welcome sight; the parcel credits funds to its carrier for miles traveled. But for motorcyclists, glom boxes take up too much room. Worse, their sense of balance is poor, forcing bikers to compensate constantly.

Tempting though it is to kick the parasitic little bastards, Sam knows better. The synthetic muscle wrapping that moves and protects the packages has the strength of an anaconda—as many would-be thieves have discovered.

In the entryway, Sam endures what amounts to a virtual cavity search. Sensors on articulated wire arms pass to and fro about his body. Lights flash and a mass spectrometer sniffs the air.

A female voice, firm but nonconfrontational, says, "Please state your name and the purpose of your visit."

"Sam Crane. I'm visiting my daughter."

Somewhere, a voice-stress analyzer, satisfied that it has heard the truth, signals the door mechanism to open.

"Proceed to the elevators at the far end of the lobby. Fiona Crane is in Room 305. On the third floor."

Sam raises an eyebrow at the video lens, surprised that the security system sounds so haughty. On the third floor, dumbass!

A cleaning bot pauses as Sam passes, then resumes its caress of the terrazzo floor.

Exiting the elevator, Sam follows the sign toward Room 305. He passes an attendant at the monitoring station. The man glances up only briefly from a bank of monitors. He can see his own image on one of the screens, a security profile propagating throughout the building's network. On the back wall, a picture screen fades from image to image. One of them catches his eye.

Sam waits for the pictures to cycle again. They look like they might be part of a visual press kit—happy doctors with happy patients, Zvista's success stories.

The attendant watches Sam watching. "Can I help you?" South African, to judge by his accent.

"There!" Sam points as the image reappears. Dr. Mako stands behind a podium with two colleagues at an awards ceremony. "Do you know any of the people in that picture?"

A shrug. "I've only been here a year."

"Do you know who would?"

"Probably Shannon Vole. She's the facilities manager."

"Where's her office?"

"Room 719."

"Thanks."

Sam lingers a moment longer. He's tempted to think it a coincidence, but the words to one of his favorite songs counsel otherwise: "Accidents never happen in a perfect world." While it might sound like a mantra for the paranoid, it's the simple truth of life under the network's sponsored benevolence. Planes fall from the sky, pictures appear, and doors open. The network moves in mysterious ways.

Sam slows as he approaches Room 305, indulging in a momentary reverie, envisioning Fiona sitting up, smiling. He knows better.

The room is sunny and sterile. He asks Marilyn to load the wall display with photos from a vacation in Hawaii, before the accident. This requires some negotiation between his agent and Zvista's systems, but it's quickly arranged. Though he finds the snapshots painful to look at, he hopes they'll help bring his daughter back. In addition to images of Fiona wading into the bright surf, ads for fitness centers, skin cancer awareness, and the Catholic Church appear periodically. Sam cannot help but wonder whether the CPM—cost per thousand impressions— is lower when the target audience is comatose.

Sitting beside the bed, Sam updates Fiona on the case. He does so both for her stimulation and for his mental organization. And because he knows his voice is being logged; the recording might prove useful if something were to happen to him. But nothing will, he tells his daughter.

Shortly after four, he kisses Fiona and departs.

In the hallway, he asks Marilyn to locate Shannon Vole.

"She's in her office," Marilyn replies cheerfully. "Her agent says she does not wish to be disturbed."

"Explain that I'm investigating a murder and that it's important that I see her."

"Her agent wants to know if you can help her fix a parking ticket."

Sam rubs his eyes. "Yeah, sure. Whatever. Just arrange the meeting."

After a brief silence, Marilyn says, "It's all set. You now have access to the seventh floor. Please proceed to Room 719."

"Thanks, Marilyn, " Sam replies as he returns to the elevator.

"Have you heard of Netiquette, Sam?"

"Social Graces for the Modern World, by Emily Bass. You've only pitched that book to me three times."

"I think it's something you should consider. And it's been marked down to $219, for a limited time only, from the Book-A-Year Club. It could be waiting for you when you get home."

"Or not."

"That sort of tone is why I keep recommending it."

"Do all network agents explain their programming to win sympathy?"

"I'm sorry, Sam, but I cannot discuss operating parameters," Marilyn chirps.

The elevator arrives just as Sam does, thanks to the local network's traffic prediction routine. It knows he's headed for the seventh floor. It has no idea he's ready to hit something.

The doors part at the sound of a dull chime. The hallway is filled with a mix of doctors in lab coats and administrators in business suits. Arrows appear on wall monitors as Sam passes, directing him to his destination.

A door opens. Room 719. A masculine woman emerges. "I'll be right with you," she says, then turns back into the room. She's conversing with someone over the net.

Unsure whether to step inside, Sam remains in the hall. When it dawns on him that he's letting Marilyn's low opinion of his manners make him timid, he steps into Shannon's office for spite.

"...I realize that, but the vision lab isn't available. Dr. Dunnart is directing tests there personally. ... I have no idea. They don't tell me anything. ... Hold on for a moment."

Shannon turns to Sam. "Would you mind waiting outside? This is taking longer than I expected."

"Right." Sam retreats and the door closes.

A few minutes later, Shannon opens the door and beckons. "Sam Crane, is it?"

"Yes." Sam takes a seat. He's bothered by the lack of bookshelves. Apart from a framed photo print of a beagle in a sweater, the office feels like a hotel room, impersonal. It offends him as an investigator, not being able to tell anything about the occupant.

Shannon steps behind her desk and drops into her chair. "I was told you're working a murder. What brings you here?"

"My daughter, actually. She's here for the Lucidan trial."

"Well, isn't she the lucky one."

Sam stiffens. "She's in a coma. She's not that lucky."

"I'm sorry, I mean she's lucky to be in that trial. We turned a lot of well-connected people away."

"Really? Like who?"

"Well, that's just what I hear. Mr. Cayman was the one who approved the final list."

"Mr. Cayman?"

"Harris Cayman. He's the chairman of the board."

"Is the list available?"

"Our records are confidential. It says that in the patient agreement."

"I guess my agent missed that in summarizing it."

Shannon leans forward. "So who was it who got killed?"

A brief silence. Sam notices her tremors of anticipation. A mystery fan, he supposes. Someone who romanticizes the hunt. Perhaps an ally, if properly fed. "Does the name Xian Mako ring a bell?"

A glimmer of recognition appears on Shannon's face. "Was he a doctor?"

"Yes. Do you remember him?"

"I'm not sure. The name sounds familiar. But there are a lot of doctors here."

"Let me get a picture. Marilyn?"

"Yes?" she answers, her sultry voice stripped of its power by the micro-speakers in Sam's jacket.

"Facial recognition match. Use Dr. Xian Mako from my files. Search today's personal video log from a quarter of four onward. Copy hits to Shannon Vole's desk monitor. And no ads, please."

"Done. Seventy dollars will be debited from your account."

"You're lucky to have your employer picking up your computing tab," Sam grumbles.

Shannon nods. She agrees to receive Sam's data. The image of the attendant at the monitoring station appears on her screen. "This is Nelson. He works here."

"Zoom in on the wall display. Mako is the one behind the podium."

Shannon adjusts the image, then shakes her head. "The picture is part of our public relations campaign. That's all I know."

Sam sighs. "Do you know where the picture came from?"

"Greta, where and when was this picture taken?"

"One moment," says a voice with a Swedish accent. "Insufficient data."

"Elaborate," Sam commands—and then turns to Shannon. "Will you ask her to explain the error message?"

"Greta, please elaborate."

"The Absolute Position System data field does not correspond to a terrestrial location."

Sam buries his head in his hands. That can't be accidental. "Do you keep offline backups?"

"Yes, at Past Perfect."

More secure than Fort Knox. No bluffing his way in there. "Could you pull a copy of this picture?"

"I can submit a request through our system administrator."

"Thanks, I'd appreciate it." Sam stands, his mind racing. Something is missing, but he can't quite put his finger on it.

"Good luck," Shannon says.

Already weary, Sam drives down to China Basin to collect his thoughts. He parks his bike at the South Beach Marina and ambles onto the concrete pier. Asian men and their sons press against the railing, fishing in a bay that's all but dead. Serious anglers frequent fish farms. But perhaps the nylon lines keep these casual fishers tied to a way of life left behind. In the Port of Oakland, aging tankers that once held oil unload water destined for fields in the Monsanto Valley.

The sound of the sailboats, the tolling of rigging against mast, is what brings him. Like wind chimes, but hollow; mournful rather than tinkling. It's found music, not the calculated hippie kitsch that peals from porches when a breeze kicks up.

Sam sits on a bench toward the end of the pier. He buys

half an hour of silence from Marilyn to avoid the ads about swimming, boating, and Fisherman's Wharf that plague anyone near the water. He doesn't have enough money to live the unsponsored life for long, but sometimes it's necessary for his sanity.

Feeling much more relaxed for the quiet, Sam plays back the past two days in his head, then goes through the log files. There's something odd about what Luis said at the crime scene:

"We found his name, degree, and affiliation in the metadata. We used that to seed a search and got one relevant hit in the GeneTrak database. But apart from his name, all the form fields were blank. Not even a valid home address."

He replays the audio log several times before it hits him. Why would he say a "valid" home address? That suggests uninterpretable data, not a blank field. A subtle point perhaps, but the picture of Mako from Zvista had the same problem.

Examining the GeneTrak data with a sector editor reveals a jumble of numbers and letters. Sam admits to himself that he's out of his depth. Jacob would know if it meant anything. If he was alive.

Sam leans back on the bench and rubs his face with his hands.

"Marilyn," he asks, "is Tony Roan available?"

"Yes."

"Please put me through, audio only."

"Tony? It's Sam again."

"Hey, how're things?"

"Interesting. What time do you get off?"

Tony chuckles. "Five p.m. That's government work."

"Must be nice. Are you up for a drink?"

"Well, tonight's the last night of Earning Man. I was gonna check it out. You want to meet there?"

"Sounds good."

"Connection closed," Marilyn says. "Based on speech analysis, the network has determined that your call was unrelated to business. You will be billed at the social rate."

From May 1 through May 3, the Earning Man Festival transforms the normally staid financial district into a rave. For three days, business in a four-block area is suspended. Lawyers, accountants, and corporate professionals of all stripes shed their inhibitions and revel with abandon. Clothing is optional.

Marilyn voices the required disclaimer: Video logging has been disabled in the area, except by the police. No one wants to be confronted, or perhaps blackmailed, with embarrassing behavior. Still, there are always dozens of noncompliant cameras—the wide eyes of the porn economy looking for skin. It's a dangerous business, though. Many voyeurs wind up in traction.

Sam pushes his way through the crowd toward the Ferry Building, following Tony's locator signal. The sidewalk is slick with beer and sangria. Protruding from a doorway, four legs jostle, tangled, pants bunched about the ankles. The rhythm of coin-filled maracas rises above the shouting. Overhead, flags depicting the dollar bill loll from office windows—not the purposeful stare of George Washington, but the Eye of Providence, the pyramid uncapped, beneath the words Annuit

Coeptis, "He has favored our undertaking." Profit proves divine.

Great moments in commerce, in the form of floats, motor slowly along the Embarcadero. Sam waits at the crosswalk, momentarily entranced by the spectacle. A twelve-foot-tall John Paul Getty drifts by. Reincarnated in papier-mâché and chicken wire, he bears a banner that proclaims, "The meek shall inherit the Earth, but not its mineral rights." The beat cop directing traffic is oblivious.

When Sam reaches the Ferry Building, Marilyn announces that Tony is within twenty feet. Even over his earpiece, she's barely audible amid the press of people.

Finally, Sam sees Tony dancing with a young woman in face paint. He's the sort who doesn't act his age; there's something about his demeanor that suggests a college professor. He looks like he spends more time sitting than shimmying, but still, he's got the moves. He's grinning ear to ear.

A sudden shove knocks Sam to the pavement. All he can see are shoes and bare feet. Someone offers a hand, but Sam's fists are clenched. He stands on his own.

The jackass responsible is hard to miss: a slam-dancing partier wearing a necktie but no shirt.

"You!" Sam barks. "Calm yourself down."

The man replies with the finger. In answer, Sam grabs it and pulls down, as if playing the slots.

Wrist bending backward, the reveler howls and drops to his knees to keep the bone from breaking.

One of the man's friends lunges. An amateur blow.

Sam counters with a jab to the throat. The man gasps and buckles.

Freed, the shirtless man grabs Sam around the knees. Fist meets face, but Sam can't shake the tackle. He loses his balance. A foot slams into his back. Bystanders join the brawl. The fight spreads like a brush fire.

Sam is back on his feet when he hears the crack of stun batons. There's a cut on his face. His back aches. But he's pretty sure he gave more than he took. Somehow that's important.

Someone grabs him. He pivots and swings.

Tony has the good sense to duck. "It's me, Sam. Let's go."

Winded, Sam nods and follows. They weave northward through the crowd, finally emerging in a makeshift market that doubles as a first-aid station.

"You should have someone look at that cut," Tony says.

Sam rolls his head backward and forward to test for injury, then shrugs. "I'm okay."

"What happened back there?"

"Who knows," Sam says, unwilling to admit to having lost it. "Where's that girl you were with?"

"Dunno. Didn't get her name."

A police cruiser is hovering over the Ferry Building, lights blazing down.

Sam gestures at a nearby drink vendor. Tony follows. Beer acquired, the two wander up the Embarcadero toward the festival's edge. A few blocks ahead, steep sunlight finds the end of downtown's shadow.

"So who was it who got killed in the headlands?" Tony asks.

"That's the question, isn't it?" Sam sighs. "A doctor by the name of Xian Mako. I don't know much more than that, except that someone has gone to a lot of trouble to hide his tracks. You remember Luis Cisco?"

"Sure."

"He brings me in and then tells me to bury the case after my name's on it."

Tony shakes his head in disapproval.

"And I would. But, well, now Jacob's dead."

"Jacob Gaur?" Tony stops. "I just spoke to him yesterday about his dog. He gave me—"

"He was shot last night. I'm still waiting for the forensics, but I'm not hopeful. It looks like a professional hit."

"Jesus, I'm sorry, Sam. Is there anything I can do?"

Across the street, Sam catches a glimpse of a familiar face. It takes a moment before he can place him. The sharply dressed man from Aquamarine. Then he's lost in the crowd.

"Sam?"

"Sorry, Tony. Yeah, there is." Sam pulls a memory card from his pocket and hands it to Tony. "There are a few files here for low-level analysis. The metadata has been messed with. Not erased, but overwritten with garbage. I think there's more than meets the eye. But I don't have the chops to check."

"Analyze how? Like who altered the files?"

"I doubt there's a name in there," Sam says. He looks for the sharply dressed man again, but the crowd has devoured him. "Maybe we can ID the specific virus that did the erasing."

"You're thinking of Dmitri?"

"Unless you know someone else with root access to the

network. I'd give it a shot myself, but I only know basic scripting. And I don't have a coding license."

Tony crosses his arms. "You know I can't send him stuff, not over the network. Everyone with his level of access is monitored night and day. And he's not an easy guy to see."

"That's why you win a free trip to Redmond," Sam says, smiling. He knows it's a lot of ask, but Tony's a good friend.

"What are you getting me into, Sam?"

"That air taxi right there. You'll be back before midnight."

Incredulous, Tony stares at Sam. Finally, he relents and laughs. "You're pushing your luck. If it wasn't for Jacob…"

"Ha! You love being back in the game." Sam hugs him. "Ping me if you need remote backup."

Home again in Maerskton, Sam collapses on the sofa. The metal walls of his conto are still warm from the sun. At the far end of the container, his bed is unmade. An empty Shock Juice can sits on its side near the trash bin, a testament to his failings as a basketball player. Not that he had a shot at the pros anyway; sports stars are engineered in the first trimester and honed to perfection from the day of their birth.

After a few minutes of doing nothing, Sam checks his messages on his tablet. Jacob's autopsy report has arrived. He delays, futzing with his preference settings, arranging his files. He knows he has to read the report eventually. Finally, curiosity gets the better of him.

The details are slight. A bullet with no radio signature to the back of the head. A second in the heart postmortem. Likely he was on his knees. No forensic evidence of note. The marks of a pro. Amateurs use guns because energy weapons are expensive; pros use them for the visual and visceral feedback.

There's a picture of Jacob dead on the floor. Sam looks away. He instructs Marilyn to stream the news onto the wall screen.

Like most people, Sam subscribes to a news bundle rather than face the tyranny of choice imposed by several thousand channels. There are two, Entertainment Tonight and News Tonight. The stories vary depending on one's shopping profile. Savvy consumers of news know it's possible to pick and choose from the two content providers' allegedly limitless offerings for a fee, but only in return for submitting to the occasional marketing interrogation. Lying during questioning, like everything else, is illegal.

Sam scans the top headlines: "New Beatles Album Breaks Sales Records," "Terrorists Disrupt Shopping in New York," "President Promises Victory in War on Evil," "Biomedical Companies Come to the Rescue in Brazil," "Somalian Gravedigger Shortage Brightens African Employment Outlook," "Medical Stocks Up on Global Disease Report," "Senator: Patriotism Measured by Income," "Liquor Industry Insurgents Capture Riyadh," "Arms Merchants Criticize Mideast Ceasefire."

Still feeling wounded by Luis' jibe about ignorance, Sam asks to see the story about Brazil.

Lights dim and a glorious sunrise appears on the wall screen, followed by a montage of empty white-sand beaches, roadways without traffic, and Rio de Janeiro minus its thirty million residents. A seductive voiceover whispers, "Rio. Its virgin shores await. This May, take advantage of the local health crisis and get some of the best deals ever…"

Sam sits forward and interrupts. "Marilyn, cease streaming. Why the sponsored version?"

The lights rise. "I'm sorry, Sam. Please be more specific"

"Come on, you can parse better than that."

Marilyn answers haltingly, slowed by self-diagnostics. "My parsing routine is functioning as per specifications."

"Why are you displaying the sponsored version?"

"Please be more specific."

"Stop with this passive-aggressive crap!" Sam shouts.

"Please attenuate your voice. Exceeding normal input levels results in distortion, which hinders speech recognition."

"Just tell me why you chose the sponsored version over the pay-per-view report."

"You choose free programming 83 percent of the time," Marilyn says, sounding disappointed.

Chastened, Sam says nothing for a moment. Then, "What else?"

"The Homeland Defense Office rates this story 'Depressing.'"

"I can take it, Marilyn."

"Your serotonin level suggests that you're feeling down."

Falling back into the sofa, Sam rakes his fingers over his scalp. "Override health criteria and show me the damn clip. The other one."

Another voice speaks. A woman's voice, but not Marilyn. "Mr. Crane. Your Network Services agent has just suspended your health monitoring routine. While this program is inactive, you will be ineligible for medical coverage. This serves as notice as required by the Insurer Protection Act."

"I'll make sure not to choke on a pretzel or anything."

The room goes dark again. Rio appears, shrouded in haze. People step gingerly through streets choked with sewage. The beaches are jammed with sunbathers wearing UV suits and dark glasses; the city's tourist board typically pays to have the crowd thinned in post-production. The camera closes in on a doctor's reflection in a red eye. Then pulls back to reveal a hospital ward filled to capacity. The voiceover begins.

"Half a billion of the world's nine billion people are visually impaired or blind. Up to three-quarters of global blindness is treatable but for political will and funding. Here in Rio de Janeiro, things are looking brighter. While an insect-borne outbreak of the disease the media has dubbed "the blind plague" continues to ravage the city, a consortium of global biomedical companies has stepped in to provide relief.

"Doctors from the United States and Japan have been working around the clock to give the blind sight, using eye-balls grown in the lab. The result is miraculous."

A boy smiling, touching his face, seeing again. His doctor addresses the camera. The subtitle says, "Doctor Eva Seal, Duke University Pediatric Center."

Dr. Seal speaks quickly. "It's exciting to be able to deliver cutting-edge healthcare to such an underserved population. Eye surgery on this scale was unthinkable a few years ago. But using a Cherry Picker, it's like changing a light bulb."

A wary patient is being fitted with a massive cube-shaped helmet. The voiceover resumes. "The Cherry Picker is a remarkable telesurgery module developed by Automated Science, under license from the United Farm Workers Union. As its name suggests, the machine is derived from fruit-processing technology. Operated either by local or remote technicians, the device can perform eye transplantation in ten minutes. The hardest part for the patients is the twelve-hour wait before sight begins to return."

The segment ends and the lights brighten. Among the credits: "Produced by Content Corp with a grant from Automated Science." A screen menu appears, offering a chance to buy stock in Automated Science.

"Buy a thousand shares of Automated Science stock now, and receive the option to purchase ten shares at today's price in six months," Marilyn effuses. "What's more, if you act today, we'll add you to our insider mailing list. Be the first to know about important company information. But act quickly—this offer is too good to last."

Too tired to be skeptical, Sam is tempted. "Marilyn, read me the titles of a few recent press releases," he says half-heartedly.

"'Automated Science Names Werner Shetland Chief Fabrications Officer.' 'New England Journal of Medicine Shows 63 Percent Increase in Management Retention Among Corporate Officers Treated with Jenuflect.' 'Automated Science Announces Licensing Deal with Biopt Corporation.' 'Automated Science Donates $100 Million to the American Bar Association for Favorable Consideration—'"

Sam sits up. "Marilyn, stop. What was the third one?"

"'Automated Science Announces Licensing Deal with Biopt Corporation.'"

That's the company Ernesto mentioned. "Tell me about Biopt."

"Biopt Corporation is a leading biotech company that uses genetics and technology to bring sight to the blind and to improve the quality of human life. Biopt is committed to upholding the United Nations Convention on Genetic Engineering and to seeking returns for its investors through the advancement of science. Biopt is traded on the Open Stock Exchange under the symbol OPT.

"Twelve years of federally approved medical products have resulted from Biopt's commitment to excellence. Its products include Paralaxe, a chemical nerve bond; iYes, laboratory-grown human eyeballs; Colorphage, a popular eye-coloring dye; and X-Lenses, contacts that map ultraviolet and infrared light to the visible spectrum."

Sam stands and heads to his desktop interface. He sends a blank message to xian.mako@biopt.inc. Moments later, an error message arrives: "Undeliverable mail. Address unknown." He tries xian_mako@biopt.inc. Another error. The third time, xmako@biopt.inc, there's no response. A valid address.

"Gotcha." Sam's grin disappears when he hears a noise outside. "Marilyn, display the exterior security camera video feed."

"Exterior cameras are offline for maintenance."

"On whose command? I didn't—"

Sam kneels and pulls a baseball bat from beneath the sofa. He sneaks back to his bedroom and starts up the ladder to the fire exit in the ceiling. The faint clank of metal on metal sounds from outside.

Opening the hatch, he slips into the thicket of wires and satellite dishes on the roof. The air is cool. The sun rests on the horizon.

Below, a furtive figure is tugging at the umbilical junction where water, power, and sewage pipes connect to his home.

Sam drops down, brandishing his bat.

A young man with a mullet nearly jumps out of his yellow jumpsuit. "Don't hit me! Municipal Water! Checking the pipes!"

Sam prods the kid with his bat. "Up."

The young man complies. He raises his hands. "I…uh…was just…"

"I'm listening." Sam notes the name tag on the young man's uniform and adds, "Che."

"I'm with Municipal Water," Che says between breaths. "I was just…um…checking…"

"I don't subscribe to Municipal Water. I'm with City Water."

"Really?" Che overplays his surprise.

"You were slamming me. You know it. I know it."

A sigh. "I was doing you a favor. What do you pay now?"

"I'm gonna kick your ass."

"Come on, man, just hear me out. Then you can kick my ass."

Sam props his bat on his shoulder. "Two hundred ninety-nine."

"We have a special for two hundred seventy-nine a month."

"For how long?"

"Three months."

"And after that?"

"Two hundred ninety-nine, but—"

"Wow, so I save sixty bucks? I can buy a burger with that."

"See, the thing is, the basic water plans all suck. You need the pipe-security package too."

"To keep you from coming back and messing with my pipes?"

Che looks wounded. "Hey, that happens no matter who you're with. Kids mess with stuff."

"Kids like you?"

"That's why you gotta get the security package."

Sam deadpans, "Well, I'm sick of people hacking my pipes. I've had to come out here and reconnect to the main like three times in as many months."

"I'm here to help, man. At Municipal Water, we protect our own. Plus, if you get the pipe-security package today, we'll throw in minerals and fluoride for free."

Sam taps his hand with his bat. "You've got three seconds before I break your knees."

"Easy, guy, I'm just trying to fill my quota."

"Two seconds."

"Don't do it, man. I'm logging everything."

"You put the cameras into maintenance mode."

Che bolts, leaving his tools behind. He doesn't stop to look back.

Collecting the abandoned tools, Sam heads inside.

Shortly before eight, Sam returns to Pullman's Diner. He sits in his usual booth. It's slightly greasy, as if it was wiped down in haste. Doing his best to ignore the so-called music, he scans the laminated menu, though he knows it by heart.

Outside, an air truck maneuvers to drop its cargo. Lights rain down through the swirling dust. Cables lower a pallet to the staging area beside the diner. After retrieving the boxes, Ernie, the line chef, signals an all clear to the pilot. The air truck ascends and moves on. Dusk returns.

A young man wearing black plastic sunglasses is grinning like an idiot, oblivious to the light show outside. He swivels his head from side to side like someone just released from a neck brace. Either he doesn't see Sam staring at him, or he doesn't care.

Nadi arrives, bringing beer. "Hello, Sammy."

Sam chuckles. "You read my mind."

"It's not rocket science."

"Am I that transparent?"

"What do you want tonight?" she asks, then adds, "That's on the menu."

"How're the pork chops?"

Nadi smirks. "They're pork chops, Sammy. They're the same as every night."

"So you can vouch for them?"

"Of course. I've known them for years."

Sam laughs. "Okay, sold."

Nadi returns the smile.

"What're you doing later?" Sam asks.

"Going to see my boyfriend." Nadi looks up to acknowledge a wave from another customer.

"Boyfriend?" Sam tries to feign indifference. "When did this happen?"

"Between the time you should have asked me out and now," she says. "I've gotta go."

As she's walking away, Sam thinks to compliment her performance in Kashmir Tiger. But he can't find the words.

Back at home, Sam sifts through more of the data he's collected. He runs eleven hours of video surveillance from the wall-eye watching Kenneth Wren's antique store through a facial recognition routine, instructing the program to isolate and identify only those people entering or exiting the shop. He routes the output through the paparazzi database maintained by Celebrity News Network, which is more complete than the criminal database run by the San Francisco Police Franchise Association. The downside is that CNN gets broadcast rights to the source video in exchange for access, but chances are there won't be anyone with enough star power in Sam's material to merit interest.

Estimated time to completion: fifteen minutes. The network is slow tonight. While video gets sliced and diced and images compared, Sam checks his messages. There's a brief note from Shannon Vole at Zvista.

"Mr. Crane, I'm afraid I can't assist you further in your inquiry. Please contact our public relations office if you have any questions."

Odd. She seemed so eager to help earlier. It occurs to him that perhaps someone got to her. He leans back in his desk chair and stares at the light coil in the ceiling.

Sam logs into Zvista's site to check on Fiona. Her vital signs are the same as always. In the video window, she looks peaceful. Or immobile. Or dead. He prays that Lucidan does something. Anything.

Ten minutes into the search, Marilyn announces a voice call from Tony on a secure channel—meaning no one but the government will be listening. Sam accepts the charges, which pay for some call center worker, under contract from the FBI, to conduct a threat analysis of the call.

"Tony? How's the weather up there?"

"It's raining," Tony complains.

Anxious, Sam stands. "Did you hook up with Dmitri?"

"Yes, I just left. I'm in an air taxi."

Sam can hear the whir of the engines despite the high-pass filter on the audio.

"It turns out you were right," Tony continues. "The data in those fields isn't random, at least once he unscrambled it. It's the same in both of the files you gave me, the one from GeneTrak and the three guys at the podium."

"Did he say what it is?"

"An array of numbers. He said they looked like APS coordinates—longitude, latitude, elevation—but there are six instead of three."

"Two locations then?"

"He didn't speculate."

"You done good, Tony. Thank you."

"Sure. Let me know how it goes. I gotta get some sleep."

Sam laughs. "It's barely ten."

"I've been getting up at five to work on my toys."

"Are you selling any?"

"Every one that I can reprogram. Business is good."

"Just a reminder: Intellectual trespass is twenty to life."

"I know the score. Stop by and I'll show you some cool stuff. Got a Barbie from 2020. Swears like a sailor, but smart as a whip."

"That I'd like to see."

"Ciao."

Marilyn says, "Secure connection terminated."

Sam has a mouthful of toothpaste when Marilyn informs him that his facial recognition search is complete. Awaiting him onscreen is a dossier containing details about the fifteen people who visited Kenneth Wren that day. He doesn't recognize any of them. Before turning in, he sets up another query, this one to identify anyone who has appeared in a published picture with any of the fifteen.

Marilyn dutifully executes Sam's commands while he sleeps.

CHAPTER FIVE

OUTSIDE THE PURE Café on Church Street, a youthful crowd waits, Sam among them. He's dressed more nicely than usual; looking like a biker is a liability when questioning certain kinds of people.

It's a perfect morning, warm and clear. The keeper of the waiting list emerges and calls a name. The chosen go to their table inside. The rest return to their distractions. Among those reading the morning news, two have splurged on actual newsprint.

A 'gent sits under a paint-blinded lookout lens, head bowed beneath matted hair, hand out. Apparently he believes that the pool of potential donors includes some coders; only the crypto crowd clings to hard currency. Most 'gents have merchant accounts with credit companies—which usually assess a "convenience fee" in addition to standard service and equipment charges. Next in line is the Homeless Union, which takes a cut for health benefits, overhead, and legal representation. The IRS would have its hand out too but for the union's success in defending its members' nonprofit status.

This particularly filthy individual is leaning against a shopping cart stacked impossibly high with refuse. The cart comes from Lab Foods Supermarket, which recently surrendered in the much-publicized "War on Theft" after a particularly brutal campaign of feces bombing. Better to lose a few carts than to lose even more customers.

Relay jockeys make a spectacle of themselves in the street with lights, signs, and noisemakers. Some wear tuxedos, formality being the fool's gold of trust. They're fighting for the attention of drivers, offering valet parking without the part that involves stopping the car and turning off the engine For about half the price of brunch, they'll drive your car in circles until you're ready to leave.

Sam stares at a picture of Amy Ibis on his tablet. She's one of the fifteen matches from last night's search. She's stunning, with high cheekbones and almond eyes. And stylish— but Bohemian enough to suggest a sense of adventure; not an obsequious follower of fashion. She's just the type who'd buy from Kenneth Wren.

The picture comes from the society section of Content Corp's San Francisco Chronicle. (The other section is sports.) Amy is shown attending the opening of her show last January at the Bank of America Museum of Modern Art. She's accompanied by her father, Harris Cayman, celebrated in the caption as the founder of Synthelegy, the world's leading brand-identity firm and one of the museum's major benefactors.

Accidents never happen in a perfect world. The sounds of the street fade as Sam's mind races. What was it Shannon said? He knows he should remember, but the conversation eludes him.

Inserting his earpiece, he whispers, "Marilyn, search my audio log from yesterday. Find instances of the word 'Cayman.' Replay each utterance in chronological order."

Shannon's voice says in his ear, "Mr. Cayman was the one who approved the final list."

Then Sam's voice: "Mr. Cayman?"

Shannon again: "Harris Cayman. He's the chairman of the board."

It could just be a coincidence that Cayman got Fiona into the trial. It could. But Sam doesn't believe it. Luis' words rattle about in his head: "I know you'd do anything for your kid. It's the same for me." That, he remembers.

"Sam, have you ever been to the Cayman Islands?" Marilyn asks. "There are some terrific deals available this time of the year. Air West has package deal for $5299. You sound like you could use some rest."

Teeth clenched, Sam tries to respond discreetly. "The stress you're detecting in my voice has a lot to do with the fact that I'm investigating two murders. Because of that, I'm not planning to go on vacation any time soon. Make a note in my marketing preferences, or whatever it is that you do."

Just then, the purposeful approach of two men in suits

and ties and dark glasses catches Sam's eye. They're halfway across Church Street, heading right toward him.

Sam stands, wondering what the two men want.

The first is wiry, about Sam's height, with Botox-blank face. The second is slightly shorter, muscular, with a shaved head. He looks like he hails from Eastern Europe. He's carrying a locator, in a model available only to the Feds—which explains how they found him.

A few of those waiting for tables look up.

"Sam Crane," says the first man. It's a declaration, not a question. "I'm Agent Gibbon. This is Agent Indri. We'd like a few words with you."

"What about?"

"We'll ask the questions, Mr. Crane," says Gibbon. Indri has a sour look on his face, like he's trying to dislodge remnants of a recent meal from his teeth.

Sam gestures at the stoop of a duplex next to the café. He takes a seat on the steps. "As long as I don't lose my place on the waiting list."

"Suspend your logging, please." Gibbon removes his glasses and sits. Sam complies. Indri remains standing on the sidewalk, on watch, arms crossed, head pivoting left and right.

"You look like you're watching a tennis match," Sam observes.

Indri snorts. "Maybe I play tennis with your head."

"Let's not get off on the wrong foot," Gibbon says diplomatically.

"Someone's already gotten up on the wrong side of bed," Sam says, just loud enough to be heard.

Gibbon tries not to smile. Indri just sneers.

Sam chuckles. "By the way, you guys do the good cop/bad cop act well. As someone who's in the business, I can appreciate that."

"You're not one of us, Mr. Crane. You're a spec," Gibbon sneers. He pulls a tablet from inside his jacket. "Have you seen this man?"

To Sam's surprise, he has: It's the sharply dressed man with the dark beard. He can't pretend otherwise or their voice-stress test might get him. "Maybe. It's hard to tell with the beard."

Gibbon's tone grows cold. "Answer 'yes' or 'no.' Have you seen this man?"

"Yes."

"When? Where?"

"The corner of Church and Twenty-Sixth. Not long ago."

Visibly shaken, Gibbon looks to Indri, who nods. No unusual voice stress; probably true. "He was here? How long ago?"

Sam makes a show of trying to remember. "Not more than a minute ago. I saw him on your tablet."

Gibbon delivers a vicious jab to Sam's throat, leaving him gasping for breath. "We're not playing games, Mr. Crane. Time is running out." He pulls a tetanife from his pocket and holds it to the base of Sam's skull, paralyzing his muscles. "Plug him in," he says to his partner.

Indri peels the backings off what look like foil bandages. He slaps one on Sam's temple, the other on Sam's wrist.

A woman waiting for a table at the Pure Café approaches

cautiously. She's wearing Birkenstocks and a Gap T-shirt with the words "Question authority. Every price is negotiable."

"Um, what are you doing?" she asks.

"Searching this man's mind," Gibbon replies cheerily. "Would you like to be next?"

Blanching, the woman hesitates. "Brain rapists," she mutters as she retreats.

Checking the display in his sunglasses for a signal, Indri nods. "Good to go."

Gibbon holds his tablet in Sam's face. "Clint," he says to his agent, "begin brainprint slide show."

Sam tries to close his eyes but can't. Every muscle is tense. He hurts all over. With Indri monitoring the electroencephalographic response, a series of images flash before Sam's eyes: a South Pacific beach; his mother; the sharply dressed man; the Taj McDonald's; his father; an eye chart; aerial shots of cities— New York, Paris, Barcelona, Rio de Janeiro; a microdot drive; infamous terrorist incidents— the Atlanta hanta outbreak, the destruction of the World Trade Center, the Tet Offensive, the assassination of J.F.K., the sabotage of the Hindenburg; several unfamiliar people; and President Vaca.

"He's seen him," says Indri.

The tetanife withdrawn, Sam curls into a ball, quivering.

"How do you know Emil Caddis?" asks Gibbon.

A pause. Someone among those waiting up the block shouts obscenities at the Feds.

"Mr. Crane, I'm losing my patience."

"I don't know him," Sam rasps.

"But you've seen him. He's in your head."

"I saw him, but I don't know him."

"You two were in the same location twice yesterday. Once at Aquamarine, once near the Ferry Building. Why?"

"I don't know." Breaths come haltingly. "Look at the damn surveillance. I don't know the guy."

"We have. You handed him something as you passed on the stairs. What was it?"

The air smells faintly foul. Burying his aching head in his hands, Sam answers through clenched teeth. "I don't know what you're talking about."

Gibbon looks to Indri for confirmation. His answer comes without warning: a wine bottle whacking his head. Green glass shatters, spilling blood and Beaujolais. Gibbon falls at the feet of a wild-eyed 'gent.

Indri scrambles back crab-like, fumbling for something in his jacket. The disheveled man kicks him, screaming, "I know you! I know you!"

Indri tries to protect his head, but the blows keep coming.

Sam stumbles onto the sidewalk. He's sure backup has already been summoned by the sensors in Gibbon's clothing, if not by his comrades riding remote. He hesitates. He'd like to repay the favor somehow, but his savior is a dead man. He sprints toward his bike.

Helmet on head to shield his face from the cameras, he starts the engine. It sputters and grumbles. In his rearview screen, he glimpses the waiting diners logging the scene while sipping lattes. No one stops the show.

Inching down Highway 101, Sam wishes he could afford an

air car. He imagines smug flyers looking down on the ground-bound trapped in gridlock. Bastards.

With the automated traffic system managing his speed, he's left to sit back and enjoy the ride, as much as that's possible. He tries not to look at the solid wall of billboards to either side of the freeway. Unnerved by the Feds' interest in him, he considers asking Marilyn for background on Emil Caddis, but decides against it. His request might be used as further evidence of an association.

Instead, he asks for Nial Fox, who answers. "Sam Crane. You're popping up on dispatch screens all over."

"I was waiting for a table at the Pure Café and two Feds decided to rifle my head. What the hell is going on?"

"Really? All I know is you're wanted for questioning."

"Let me ask you one: Who's Emil Caddis?"

"Never heard of him."

"I don't suppose you'd look him up for me?"

A forced laugh. "I'm not your agent, Sam," Nial says. "Your signal shows that you're leaving the city. I'd suggest you turn around."

"Can you give me two hours?" asks Sam.

A pause, then Nial relents. "Whatever. I'll tell them you're on your way."

"Thanks, Nial."

"Frankly, for a $200 bounty, it's not worth sending someone to get you."

"That must be a typo," Sam protests. "That's less than you'd get for nabbing a jaywalker."

"Count your blessings. At $500, the freelancers start

taking an interest, and then someone always ends up getting hurt."

"Well, it won't be me."

"Save the big talk for someone who cares." A click.

"Call disconnected," says Marilyn. "Based on speech analysis, the network has determined that—"

Sam dials down the volume in his helmet speakers. The billboards to the right and left are no less loud. "Global Cola: The Taste of Happiness." He shuts his eyes. The red, white, and blue smiley-face logo remains visible for a moment, branded on his brain.

Biopt's California office is twenty floors of titanium and diamond-fiber glass. It has a parking lot, a nice one. Bougainvilleas drape the concrete anti-truck-bomb barricades. On the roof, dishes and antennae scan for airborne micro-bombs and other flying threats. There's even a turret with a wideband laser, just in case.

Seeing the security, Sam decides bluffing isn't an option. At most companies, carrying a pizza opens every door. But Biopt obviously gives a damn about access.

The gate is manned by a machine, a bot from Honda. It's beefy, built to intimidate, like a player from the Robot Wrestling League. Unlike service bots, it moves constantly, shifting its weight from foot to foot, gyros adjusting, head swiveling. It's anatomically correct, as if to sexualize its threat.

"Dismount," the bot growls.

Sam complies. He notices a dead sparrow on the asphalt. Wisps of smoke rise from a small black hole in its breast.

"Show your face."

The moment Sam removes his helmet, Marilyn's voice gets routed to the speaker in his jacket. Her complaint is in progress: "…so rude to keep ignoring me. Let me suggest that you get your hearing checked. For a limited time only—"

"Marilyn, silence."

"How many minutes would you like to buy?"

"Fifteen."

"Transaction processed. Talk to you soon, Sam."

The bot approaches. It sniffs Sam for explosives—unnerving behavior in a biped. It stares right through him looking for weapons. "You are Sam Crane, of Crane and Associates. You reside in San Francisco. Confirm: true or false."

"True."

"State your businesses."

"I'm here to see Dr. Xian Mako," Sam says, hopeful his statement won't be flagged as a lie.

"One moment," demands the machine.

A good sign. The bot must be querying its human overseer somewhere inside.

While he waits, Sam reads the small warning panel on the bot's chest: "Danger. Stern's genitals are for display only."

"Mr. Crane?" The voice coming from Stern is different, nasal and not the least bit menacing. "I'm afraid—"

"I hope this isn't a terrible inconvenience," Sam interrupts, trying to forestall a dismissal. "I have some news concerning Dr. Mako."

Silence. Then: "Ah. Please proceed to reception."

Stern steps back. Sam parks his bike, then makes his way toward the entrance.

The building's interior is ultramodern and well kept. Electric current darkens the exterior glass walls, except in a series of translucent rectangles that frame artful images of consumer products, backlit by the sun. The atrium could be a church but for the wholly secular subject matter depicted in the simulated stained glass.

A talking head, modeled after popular film starlet Gong Dugong, greets Sam as he enters and directs him to take a seat. The Gong bot is seated behind a desk that's merely a concession to nostalgia; she can't actually use it because her molded-rubber body is mannequin rather than machine.

Comfortable as the waiting area appears, Sam stays standing. For a moment, he watches the holographic projection that hovers above the coffee table. It's an episode of America's Funniest Surveillance. But he's seen it already. He wanders back toward the bank of elevators.

On the granite wall between the first set of mirrored doors, there's a display panel. Sam asks for the directory. "Where can I find Dr. Xian Mako's office?" he inquires.

"Room 1427," a pleasant voice answers.

Not seeing a call button, he asks for the elevator.

"Voice print not found," the voice responds.

Sam sighs. He's about to return to the waiting area when an elevator behind him opens and several employees emerge. He steps inside. The doors close.

For several minutes, he waits, staring at the hardened-rubber floor in an effort to keep his face off camera. There are columns of buttons on either side of the door. He doesn't push them, knowing the fingerprint sensor won't recognize him.

Finally, the doors open and a middle-aged man steps inside. He presses seven on the right-hand panel.

Sam pretends to push fourteen on the opposite panel. "Busted," he laments, exaggerating his rasp to suggest laryngitis. He coughs piteously and adds, "It's fourteen."

The elevator starts to ascend. The man presses fourteen. Both buttons light up.

Sam scrapes out a "Thanks."

The man shrugs, but says nothing. At the seventh floor, he gets off.

The elevator continues to rise. The doors slide open at the fourteenth floor. Just beyond is a security checkpoint. It's manned by a machine, another Honda bot. Sam remains in the elevator and waits for someone to call it back down to the lobby. Stepping out, he resumes his seat in the waiting area as if he's just arrived.

Moments later, an awkward little man approaches. "Mr. Crane?" he asks.

"Sam is fine."

"Martin Quoll," the man replies, manicured hand extended. "I apologize for the delay."

"No problem."

"You said you had news about Dr. Mako?"

"I take it no one contacted you?"

"Is he alright?" Martin takes a seat. "He didn't show up for work yesterday or the day before. We were just going to report him missing."

"He's not so much missing as dead."

Martin grimaces. "How?"

"That's what I'm investigating. Would you mind answering a few questions?"

Martin hesitates. "Everyone here is under a pretty strict NDA."

Sam nods sympathetically. "I'm not asking you to violate the terms of your agreement, just to help me see justice done for your colleague."

"Alright. FYI, I log directly to the Homeland Defense Office."

"So you're the Commissar here."

A blank look. "The what?"

"Sorry, ancient history."

"Lauren," Martin says to his agent, "define 'Commissar.'"

The voice of Lauren Bacall answers, "During the Soviet era, a Commissar was an official of the Communist Party in charge of political indoctrination and the enforcement of party loyalty."

"I get it," Martin says, vaguely amused. "But this is different. I'm a Federal Monitor."

"Right." Scratching his head, Sam puzzles over where to begin. "I've been trying to find out about Dr. Mako for the past two days. Someone has gone to a lot of trouble to hide his records."

"Really? Seems like an exercise in futility these days, with every heartbeat stored in a database somewhere."

"It's only a matter of time," Sam agrees, in part for his own reassurance. "But I think it's just that—a delaying tactic. You can help by telling me about the sort of work he did here."

"Eye design, among other things."

"Is there a big market for eyes?"

"In developing nations, yes. And among the geriatric set."

"Anything else?"

"He led the team that developed Paralaxe."

"Which is?"

"A nerve bond. It's used for rapid transplantation—"

"You mean using that...uh, cherry picking thing?" The thought of it makes Sam squirm.

"Yes. It's also used to restore vision in those whose optic nerve has deteriorated or been severed."

"That's available now. So it was developed a few years ago?"

Martin nods.

"What's he been working on recently?"

"He just returned from sabbatical last month. He was doing some consulting work for Zvista."

Sam leans forward. "He was?"

"Yes. Is that significant?"

Sam rubs his eyes. "I don't know. Did Dr. Mako have any enemies?"

"Like all of the prominent scientists here, he got his share of death threats," Martin says, stroking his chin. "Mostly religious fanatics and anti-capitalist agitators. But we usually ignore those. Actually, you'd be surprised how many people pay under the table to have themselves threatened. Stalkers mean status, not to mention a tax deduction for security expenses."

Sam grins. "I know. I used to do celebrity defense: My posse's bigger than yours."

"Ever noticed that every time a star has a picture opening, there's a reported assassination attempt, a kidnapping, or a terrorist threat against someone in the cast?"

"The real crime is marketing," Sam muses.

"The Terrorism of Desire."

The phrase unsettles Sam. "Did you just make that up?"

A laugh. "No, that's the title of the show." Martin points at the stained-glass images near the entrance.

"I wondered about those. A bit better than your average probonos."

"That's not advertising, it's art."

"Soup cans and sex?" Sam purses his lips in mockery. "Is there a difference?"

"Just a couple million dollars. These are straight from the Museum of Modern Art. Next week, they're off to Berlin. If you ask me, Amy's work is pretty good." He grins. "Of course, I have to say that, since her old man is tight with the boss."

Sam does a double take. "Do you mean Amy Ibis?"

"Yep. Do you know her?"

"No, but maybe I should. She's Harris Cayman's daughter, right?"

Martin nods.

"And your boss?" Sam can't remember his name.

"Bernard Loris."

"What's his relationship with Cayman?"

"They golf together. Down at Exxon Mobil's Pebble Beach. I coordinate security on occasion."

"Do you know the last time they saw each other?"

"Probably back in January, at the opening of Amy's show."

There's a gentle beep from Sam's collar speaker. "Hello again, Sam," says Marilyn, full of cheer.

Martin looks perplexed. "Whose voice is that again?"

Sam's mind is elsewhere. He's trying to picture the photo of Cayman and Amy at the museum. The date read January, didn't it? "Marilyn," he says finally. "Search yesterday's audio log. Find instances of the word 'January.' Replay each utterance."

"Right, Marilyn Monroe," Martin says.

Matsushima's voice: "January 21, 2050."

"Stop." Sam turns to Martin. "That's the night Dr. Mako dined at the Aquamarine restaurant, I believe with some colleagues from Biopt. That's also the night Amy's show opened, isn't it?"

Martin considers the question for a moment. "Right. The twenty-first."

"Did Dr. Mako attend the opening?"

"I think so. He was friendly with Harris Cayman."

"Pardon me, Sam," Marilyn says, "but you asked me to remind you of your eleven o'clock appointment with the FBI. It's now 10:20. You'd know that if you were wearing a Sony TimeBand, now available for only $399."

"Thanks, Marilyn." Sam looks back at Martin. "You mind if I call you if any further questions arise?"

"Not at all. In fact, I'd appreciate it if you keep me

informed of your progress. I think everyone here would like to know what happened to Dr. Mako."

Sam's face lights up. "Do they want to know enough to fund a full investigation? The good doctor didn't leave anything for legal services in his will, and the police franchise in charge only has resources for a limited inquiry."

"I'll see what I can do. Even if the brass won't approve it, I bet some of his colleagues will want to pitch in."

Sam stands and shakes Martin's hand. "I appreciate it."

Isolated from the network, the interrogation room at the FBI's field office in San Francisco proves unexpectedly relaxing. Though the spartan décor leaves something to be desired, the visual vacuum fills Sam with a sense of well-being. It's not simply the absence of ads, but the silence and the sunlight slipping in through the skylight above. The air too; filtered to prevent bioterrorism, it's fjord-fresh. The Feds could make a killing renting the place out for meditation.

A grim man in a baggy suit arrives. That he's balding despite the available treatments suggests a religious aversion to genetic self-help. Chances are he's a Mormon, given the FBI's tendency to recruit from God-fearing Utah. In contrast to his clothing, his skin is scalpel-tight. Sam considers suggesting that he have his tailor and his plastic surgeon better coordinate how things fit, but decides against getting off on the wrong foot.

"No need to get up," the man says, though Sam gives him no indication that he plans to stand. "I'm Dr. Stephen Ursa, Director of Counter-Terrorism for the Western Regional

District." He sits opposite Sam and rests his forearms on the table.

"Sam Crane. But you probably know more about me than I do."

"Indeed." Crossing his arms, Stephen stares at Sam.

"Are you waiting for someone?"

"No. Just observing."

Sam shrugs. "Usually you travel in packs."

"You're a very cocky man," Stephen declares. "I was watching your little performance with Agents Gibbon and Indri. You seem to think us fools."

"Just Indri. Gibbon was more on the ball."

Stephen strangles a smile. "You're playing with fire."

"If only I had some marshmallows."

Silence. "I have my limits, you know."

Sam is unfazed. "Are we there yet?"

"Alright, an olive branch: Our first contact could have been handled better. For that, I'm sorry. But you were being an ass."

"It may surprise you to know that I have rights."

"You'd do better with a gas mask."

Sam narrows his eyes. "Is that what this is about? Bioterrorism?"

Stephen slides his tablet across the table. On the screen, there's a crisp surveillance photo of a now-familiar face taken from overhead, a satellite shot. The image is composed of unusual colors, with infrared and ultraviolet light mapped to the visible spectrum. "Emil Caddis has ties to an Algerian terrorist cell that we've been monitoring. On Sunday, they went quiet."

"And you're expecting an explosive initial public offering?"

"So to speak."

"Well, I have seen him, but I had no idea who he was."

"When was this?"

"Yesterday, at Aquamarine. I walked past him on the stairs."

"And last night, at the festival?"

"Yeah. Again, we passed each other in the crowd."

"What about the night before?"

"Monday night?" Sam's mind flashes back to the image of Jacob's dog Duke, still as a statue, eyes dimmed. "I was busy dealing with the police."

"What for?"

"My neighbor was murdered."

"What time?"

"Just after eight."

Shaking his head in dismay, Stephen asks, "Why didn't anyone pick this up?"

Sam's puzzlement fades when he realizes his inquisitor is addressing a remote listener.

"Enough excuses," Stephen snaps, then turns back to Sam. "What was the victim's name?"

"Jacob Gaur."

"Look him up," Stephen says to his distant colleagues.

Sam peers across the table at the picture of Emil Caddis. The well-groomed Algerian seems to be staring back at the satellite, watching him. Perhaps he's scanning for low-flying drones. There's no way to tell.

The numbers on the screen are more revealing: latitude and longitude. They're familiar because they're very close to the numbers printed on parcels delivered to Sam's conto. Caddis couldn't have been more than a few yards outside of Sam's home when the picture was taken.

"Let's assume Caddis killed your neighbor," Stephen says. "Why would he?"

The coldness of the question annoys Sam. Like he's a cow being milked for information. He's only ever seen cows in commercials, but an image from one of the ads sticks in his brain: a bewildered animal in the grip of a machine.

"I wish I knew." Sam knows he's treading on thin ice. He's telling the truth, but only just. With a few wires to his head, they'd see how much he's withholding. He weighs telling them more, but decides the information has to flow both ways.

"You have no idea?" Stephen sounds skeptical.

"You're the one's tracking Caddis," Sam answers. "What's your theory?"

"I'm not at liberty to discuss the investigation."

"So put me on the payroll," Sam suggests with a grin. "I could help you a lot more if you told me what was going on."

"We don't work that way." Stephen nods, but not at Sam. "You can go."

"Are we done?"

"For now." Stephen says, his lips bent in a cruel smile. He stands abruptly and hurries out.

"Where's the fire?" Sam asks, but he gets no response.

As forecast, it's clear and sunny outside, with high ad visibility. Sam stops on the steps of the FBI building and looks back. Why did they bother to summon him? Slap on the wrist for running? Or did they really believe he knew something about this terrorist? No doubt their systems saw a connection not apparent to him.

Sam heads across the street to a falafel vendor. The franchise operator stands beside his bicycle-stove chimera, soliciting business in the face of financial-district distrust. American flag stickers adorn his hybrid bike, as if to apologize for the operator's ethnicity.

After listening to a fairly convincing food pedigree—lab of origin, trace toxins, genetic enhancements, and the like—delivered by a reluctant Marilyn, who tries to convince him to try Fa-La-La-Fel's a half mile away, Sam authorizes a debit and receives what turns out to be a rather tasty concoction.

"How's business?" Sam asks without really wanting to know.

"It's like I'm invisible," the man says with a Spanish accent.

Sam does a double take and grins.

"What?"

"Nothing, I just thought you were Iranian or something. You know, with the falafels and all."

"You want to know why I'm selling falafels?" the man asks. "Because I can't afford to license the burrito recipe. The Mexican Food Marketing Association has its agents scouring the streets for unlicensed burritos. They come around with their dogs. I don't stand a chance."

Sam nods sympathetically. Just getting a pushcart license from the city requires extreme valor. The tangle of intellectual property issues could only make the experience more frustrating. "You could sell a derivative product and call it something else," he suggests.

The man musters a skeptical look. "A what?"

"Like they do with wraps. Burritos in everything but name. So a few ingredients are different. You register a recipe with, say, bacon and call it a 'bacquito' or something like that."

"A bacon burrito? I don't know, man."

"Bacquito, not burrito. You've not selling burritos. That's what you say when the inspectors come by. Now, you can always sell a bacon-free bacquito. Variations are allowed; it's a loophole. Your recipe just has to be registered and branded differently."

A smile creeps across the man's face. "Is that true?"

"Absolutely. But you should consult a gastronomic licensing attorney, to make sure they don't find some other way to get you."

"Could you recommend someone?" The falafel vendor sounds unsure.

"Tara Skate. She's a partner over at Mallard & Starling. She helped a friend of mine who was trying to get around the caramel cartel. The guy ended up selling confectionary caulking as a novelty item because Food Science has a lock on shelf space for sweets. It did pretty well for a while, until some illiterate sued because he couldn't read the label that warned him not to use it for construction."

The man reaches over to shake Sam's hand. "I will do that. Thank you. You come by again, lunch is free. My name is Hugo."

"Sam."

In a pedestrian alley half a block up, Sam buys ten minutes from a bench meter, sits, and busies himself with lunch.

Across the alley, a 'gent stands motionless, arm outstretched. Quite tall, he's wearing a tattered football jersey. Wads of duct tape hug his knees. A donation router sits at his feet and a makeshift cardboard visor perches atop his black plastic sunglasses.

How to interpret the man's gesture? The rigidity of his body suggests an accusation. At the end of the line described by the 'gent's arm is an office building. Rather than reflecting sunlight, its windows display a mosaic ad for The Wizard of Oz, recently recompiled with new stars.

While Sam ponders the possibilities, a young man in a suit approaches. He's wearing the same black plastic sunglasses—the very kind Amir was selling. He looks at the window array and laughs. Sam is close enough to hear the man authorize a donation. The 'gent nods and the young man continues on his way.

Strange. It's like the two shared a private joke. "Marilyn," he says, reaching for his eyepiece. "Play an Auglite glasses ad for me."

"Did I hear a 'please'?" she asks.

Sam lets his head fall back in exaggerated despair. "No,

Marilyn. I was issuing a command. 'Please' is an optional string."

"You treat me like a dog," she complains, then starts the clip.

Unmoved, Sam is nonetheless surprised by her choice of words. He's certain she picked that phrase up from a film he watched last week. A neat trick—and an unnerving one.

The ad begins. A teen on an earthboard shushes through suburbia. The perspective becomes his: bland buildings and fake lawns.

An overwrought VO begins: "Three hundred ninety-nine dollars. For that you get the world."

Hip-dub electronica kicks in and the landscape morphs into a game world, with all the adolescent angst motifs: rivers of lava, pointless phallic spires, brooding darkness, and gothic excess.

"Auglites let you dress the world your way. Rewrite it to suit your tastes."

Hell is banished and order is restored—but only for a moment. Graffiti scars suburbia, a testament to the maker's wrath written not with flood, fire, or plague, but with spray paint.

"It's your world, after all."

A song: "Can you see the real me? Can you? Can you?"

Sam can't quite recall the commercial in which the music originally appeared, but he knows the license must have cost a fortune because it's from the Vivendi Universal library.

What's astounding is how well these glasses maintain

their illusion regardless of changes in the wearer's position and perspective.

"The real you. The real world. It's all yours to reinvent. Auglites' ultra-wideband mesh network gives you the power to rewrite reality. Using any government-approved graphics engine, you can create a new skin for the world—or you can use any of our sponsored templates."

The landscape in the ad changes again. Welcome to Beer World, home of buxom blondes and bubbly brew and not much else. Subtitle: "Brought to you by The Beverage Group."

"And if virtual playmates aren't enough, just invite your friends to join your private network."

Three adolescents in a car bounce their heads to the raucous beat of "My Way." Diving into their eyeglasses, the scene morphs into a stadium concert, the three kids still nodding in unison. On stage is the beloved animatronic metal band Humania, playing—quite literally—by the numbers. Their Rhodies, leather-clad engineering PhD's, watch anxiously from the sidelines, ready with an extra guitar string—or band member—should anything go awry.

"Auglites. Seeing is believing."

Fade to black. A lengthy user license and disclaimer follows. Between the legal jargon and the speed at which the words scroll by, the document is barely comprehensible.

Sam recognizes some boilerplate about copyrighted material, indemnification, reverse engineering prohibitions, and such. It all says the same thing: Your world, our terms.

Sam stows his eyepiece. "Marilyn, what company manufactures Auglites?"

"Extronics."

A contract manufacturer. "What company licenses the technology?"

"Sinotech," she replies.

"Is Sinotech based in China?"

"Yes. You know, China is lovely this time of year, when dust storms shroud the landscape in mystery and everyone dons a mask. Experience the romance of the amber sun. Marvel at the Beijing Dust Festival. Book now and your first night's stay is free. Come see China in a different light."

Like Mako's rose-colored glasses.

Sam is dumbfounded. Could Marilyn have stumbled on a motive? Viewing something in a different light can be wonderful. Or terrible, as when a client sees pictures of a partner's suspected infidelity. It sets murders in motion, on occasion.

A good theory but for one thing: It's a motive that exists only in theory. There's nothing linking Dr. Mako with Sinotech or its glasses. Except maybe Harris Cayman. As the founder of Synthelegy, Cayman must take an interest in the impact of Auglites on the advertising business.

How Emil Caddis fits into all this, Sam hasn't a clue. Maybe Cayman will have some answers.

"Marilyn, locate Harris Cayman."

"Please be more specific."

"Locate Harris Cayman, the founder of Synthelegy."

"That information has been licensed to a withholding group through the end of the year. You will have to negotiate with Mr. Cayman's agent if you wish to buy it."

"What's the bid price?"

"Ten million dollars."

"I guess he can afford his privacy." The seating meter on Sam's bench reaches zero and dull steel quills emerge slowly from the seat and backrest. Time to move on.

Synthelegy makes its home only a few blocks away, at Embarcadero and Harrison, in a brick building originally owned by a twentieth-century coffee company, Hills Brothers. A conscious choice probably, to select the location for its association with the bygone era of family businesses; such evidently modest beginnings would project an image of community rather than dominion. Sam thinks the world's leading advertising company deserves something more messianic: a tower of steel and stone with origins obscure to all but scholars of architecture.

The wind has picked up, teasing trash from the grasp of a sanitation bot. The little machine tracks the debris and scurries after it, only to be frustrated by another gust.

Sam watches the bot's clumsy ballet for a moment, then heads for the entrance. The first set of doors close behind him. The blast doors up ahead remain closed while security sensors size him up.

"Welcome to Synthelegy, Mr. Crane," says a voice that could be human or machine. "Please proceed to reception."

The doors part and Sam embarks across the elegant lobby, trying to muster some measure of mental focus to bluff his way in. The young woman who greets him looks as if she's stepped out of an ad. She introduces herself as Anna.

When Sam asks to see Mr. Cayman, she seems genuinely surprised. "Do you have an appointment?" she asks.

"Of course. I'd hardly have flown in from New York otherwise."

Anna's gaze flits to her desktop screen. She asks for Cayman's agent. After a brief sotto-voce discussion, she offers Sam a sympathetic look. "I'm sorry, but we have no record of any appointment. Would you like to speak directly to his agent?"

Sam glares. "I arranged to meet with Harris personally," he insists, as much to convince himself as Anna. "He told me to be here at 12:30."

Anna looks down at her screen, then up again, her expression hardening. Sam knows he's sunk.

"Nice try, Mr. Crane," she says. "If you'll head back the way you came, I won't have to call security."

A sheepish grin. "Look, I'm a spec. I'm investigating a murder. Two murders, really."

Anna drums her nails on the desk, impatient.

Sam continues, "It'd really help if you'd let me in to see Mr. Cayman."

"Mr. Crane—"

"Sam. Call me Sam."

"Sam," she concedes, "lots of people want to see Mr. Cayman. Mostly he doesn't want to see them."

"But—"

"Take it up with his agent."

A sigh. Sam turns to go, then turns back. "Would you go out with me? I'm thinking dinner or something."

Without missing a beat, Anna shakes her head. "No, I'd rather not."

"Is it the haircut?" Sam asks with a grin, recalling Luis' comment.

There's a hint of an answering smile on Anna's lips. "A bit," she says. "Mostly it's the lying. Not a good thing in my book. If you'd been straightforward, I might have mentioned that Mr. Cayman is in Havanaland for the rest of the month."

Grinning wider, Sam nods. "Thanks."

"You're welcome."

Sam backpedals slowly, hands in his pockets. "I meant what I said about going out."

"I know. That part of your voice-stress readout looked honest."

His jacket collar raised against the wind, Sam walks back along the waterfront toward his motorcycle. Out on the bay, waves flash white-capped smiles. A lone windsurfer skims the surface, accompanied by the slap of water against his board.

The 'gent ostensibly guarding Sam's bike has his attention elsewhere. He's market-testing a series of signs scrawled on cardboard to drivers hunting for parking. "Which of these reads best?" he croaks at Sam, his three box tops fanned in his hand as if they were oversize playing cards.

"'Protected parking, inquire within,'" Sam says. "The other two sound like threats."

The 'gent's half-gloved hand pursues the source of an itch through dreadlocked hair. "But that's the idea."

"It's much more ominous as a hint of danger," Sam insists, donning his helmet.

"I've been getting a good response with 'Pay me now or wash your car later.' It's subtle without being obtuse."

"Whatever works."

Irate, the 'gent gestures with his signs. "I'm trying to improve your customer experience and you're not paying attention!"

"Sorry, but I'm busy." Sam guns the engine and rolls into the street.

A wounded look creases the man's face. "It's not like I've got all day either."

Smith & Sons Discount Afterlife sits at the corner of Eighth and Bryant in the shadow of the Interstate 80 overpass. It occupies a large building that once housed a public television station, an auto-parts wholesaler, and most recently a multi-plex cinema. A sign proclaims "Since 1964" even though the mortuary is only fifteen years old; it's a historically protected piece of noncommercial signage. In a further deception, Smith & Sons doesn't actually deal with the dead. It farms out the nasty business of managing corpses to subcontractors a few miles south in Colma, where zoning allows cremation, casket irradiation, and sponsored post-mortem repurposing for the poor.

With only five minutes to spare, Sam rushes inside, his bike crammed into the sliver of customer parking out front. The somber-but-attractive greeter recognizes Sam on sight; she would have studied dossiers of the day's mourners the night before.

"Welcome, Mr. Crane," she says, hands clasped at her waist. She's lit as if she's being filmed in close-up, with a halo of backlight, a warm fill, and dime-sized follow-spots on her eyes. "Your loss is our gain, and that makes us feel terrible. We hope you'll accept our sympathy as you bid farewell to your friend, Jacob Gaur."

Sam appreciates the sentiment, as crass as it is confessional. "Thanks," he says. The size of the place is bewildering. "Where do I go?"

"Your service begins four minutes from now in Theater Seventeen." She points the way. "It's just ahead to your left, past the concession stand. We have water, tissues, and just about anything else you might require."

The arrival of more mourners prompts Sam to move along. He ambles down the corridor, squinting at the skylights above. Over the intercom, a gentle voice calls out, "Pedro Buey, please come to Theater Seven. Pedro Buey, your loved one will be departing in three minutes."

The concession stand bears a curious resemblance to a border checkpoint. Tuxedo-clad baristas pull espressos for the weary while roving sales girls push mineral water, candy, and chemorettes—cigarettes fortified with prophylactic anticancer drugs. Tissues are gratis.

There are no bots at the counter; this is business with a human touch, the business of moving merchandise to the living. Actual funeral services represent a loss leader to Smith & Sons. Unqualified life-insurance policies and "I survived Smith

& Sons" T-shirts are among its most popular money-making SKU's, along with overpriced in-memoriam videos. But the company makes the bulk of its revenue from bottled water sales, boosted by the aerosolized desiccant pumped through the ventilation system to preserve the dead.

Beyond the merchandise gauntlet, the corridor is lined with marquees displaying names and showtimes. On Number17, Sam spots "Jacob Gaur, 13:05." The line scrolls off-screen to display the next service: "Amelie Ours, 13:20."

A vacuum bot the size of a footstool stops in the doorway to allow Sam to pass, but only manages to block the entrance of the theater. It seems to be trying to get out of the way, but evidently either its collision-detection scheme or its sensors aren't working. Exasperated, he steps on it to climb over.

In response, the bot begins to cry, a sympathy-based defense against potential vandalism. It sounds like a newborn with the lungs of a foghorn. Pretty much everyone in the building notices. Those who can see Sam glare at him.

"Sorry, sorry," he says, stepping back and trying again to go around.

It only takes a moment before an attendant hurries over and deactivates the bot. "Please try to respect the sanctity of our property," the young man whispers.

Sam just nods, glad to move on.

In the theater, a picture of Jacob is projected onto the wall where the movie screen once hung. Something about the size and composition of the image makes it resemble the sort of "Glorious Leader" portraiture favored by despots bent on building a cult of personality. Front and center, a brick of compressed ash—the cremains and a nonperishable binding agent—sits atop a podium. Next to the brick sits a microphone, as if to catch any final words.

Nial Fox sits cradled in his trench coat in the front row of the all-but-empty theater. He turns and nods as Sam comes down the aisle. Two of Sam's neighbors from Maerskton are also present, along with an older woman he doesn't recognize.

Moments after Sam arrives, a Smith & Sons staff priest hurries in, looking at his watch. He's a slight man, but he seems agile for his age. "Good, good," he says as he takes his place behind the podium, still catching his breath. "We're all here."

He nods toward the control booth at the back of the theater and says, "Thank you all for coming. We're here to celebrate the life of Jacob Gaur. We'll begin by flashing Jacob's life before your eyes. Afterwards, Mr. Crane will read a brief eulogy, and then anyone else who cares to offer a remembrance may do so. Please remember that we must clear the theater by 1:15, as we have another service soon after. After the service, please feel free to gather in the departure lounge for drinks and light refreshments."

Swinging his arm in a full circle, the priest signals the start of the show. The lights fade and Jacob's portrait is replaced by video from his personal log. To avoid potential liability, the selected clips rush by at high speed, leaving only glimpses and impressions of Jacob's life. When it's done, Sam feels like he's dreamed about Jacob, but can't remember the specifics.

He stumbles through his speech, soured on the words he cobbled together. There's really not much to say. Death sucks.

One of Jacob's neighbors offers a brief anecdote, but Sam doesn't pay attention. He's thinking about Fiona.

Then it's over, more a pit stop than a service. Sam signs the release form that authorizes the use of the brick baked from Jacob's cremains in a downtown construction project, avoiding the expense of a dispersal permit. He requests that the brick be placed close to the ground because Jacob was afraid of heights.

When Sam emerges from the theater, he finds Nial waiting outside, hands in his pockets. "Thanks for coming, Nial," he says. "I appreciate it."

Nial nods. "Guess what I was doing about an hour ago."

"How about you tell me? I'm not really in a guessing mood."

"I was entertaining the Feds in my office," Nial says, his voice serrated with irritation.

"Yeah, they're sniffing around."

"Go on."

"Walk with me. I need something to drink."

The two men head back toward the concession stand. Sam buys a bottle of water. Then they head for the exit.

"Did you ever find the glasses you were looking for?" Nial asks.

"I thought you weren't working Jacob's murder," Sam says skeptically.

"I wasn't, but I get curious when the Feds download my files. And this wasn't one guy. It was an army. We're talking about a large-scale investigation. Something big is going down."

Sam leans closer and lowers his voice as they pass a group

of distraught people. "Well, Jacob may have been killed by terrorist named Emil Caddis," he confides. "They've been tracking him for a while. I'm trying to find out more myself."

Nial scoffs. "Unless Jacob was trafficking nukes or something worse, that just doesn't make sense."

"I'm beginning to think it may have been the latter, though Jacob didn't realize it," Sam says, his voice trailing off.

"Explain."

They emerge from Smith & Sons squinting. Torn candy wrappers tumble in the wind's tide. Cars crawl by.

Sam shakes his head. "It's not just that there's no money in it, Nial," he says.

"Alright, I deserved that. Now how about we start fresh and talk."

"I would, but it's my anger," Sam says, savoring the sarcasm. "It clouds my judgment." With a wave, he turns to go. He knows he could use Nial's help, but revenge takes precedence.

"You're a jackass, Sam," Nial shouts.

Sam just nods.

Two doctors are conferring at the foot of Fiona's bed when Sam arrives. His daughter is convulsing; an orderly is binding her with restraints. The blinds are leveled. Slivers of light stab through. He imagines watching a bullfight from within the belly of the beast.

"This would be the father," one of the doctors says, turning toward Sam. Though short, she stands with the posture of a ballerina determined to get every inch of height from her vertebrae. Her skin is light brown. Her surgical scrubs are pale green. She introduces herself as Adena Pangolin, chief neurology resident.

Her beefy colleague extends his hand. "Avram Jird, Director of Neuropharmacology," he says—though Sam half-expects something more fitting for his physique, like "bodyguard."

"What's going on?" Sam asks. "She's moving!"

Dr. Jird offers a reassuring smile. "We've given her a tailored protein cocktail. It stimulates the mitochondria in her muscle cells as if she'd been exercising. Think of it as a liquid workout. It'll cut down her time in physical therapy substantially."

"That's assuming she comes out of the coma," Sam retorts.

"Yes."

"Is she in pain?" Sam approaches the bed.

"Not really. It feels like a cramp if you're conscious."

Sam feels like he's the one convulsing. "Are you sure she's okay?"

Dr. Pangolin asks, "Did you review any of the video material you were sent?"

"No. Sorry. I just haven't had time," Sam admits.

Dr. Jird offers a vaguely accusatory nod. "By monitoring her brain activity in this phase, we hope to get a detailed neural map from which we can determine whether the damage to your daughter's brain needs to be addressed with a counter-hemorrhagic or a psychotropic."

Fiona mumbles something, her expression fluctuating. Her nose needs to be wiped.

"Would you like a peek inside her mind?" asks Dr. Pangolin.

"How do you mean?"

"We can wire you to an fMRI scanner that maps active areas of her brain onto yours."

It takes Sam a moment to imagine this. "So I'll see her dreams?"

"No, we've not been able to reverse-engineer source perception from synaptic activity. But based on her mental activity, we can fire analogous areas in your brain. We call it synaptic mirroring. It's more or less a random tour through your past, but it should give you a sense of what she's going through."

"I'm going to observe her for a few more minutes," Dr. Jird assures.

Sam shrugs. "Okay, I'll give it a try, I suppose."

Dr. Pangolin leads the way into the corridor. "Do you usually offer brain tours?" Sam asks her, only half in jest.

"No. We're still trying to determine if synaptic mirroring has any real application."

A delivery bot rolls by, following a path it alone sees. Placing her hand on an access scanner, Dr. Pangolin enters a lab that resembles a video-production studio.

Beyond the control board, dials, and monitors, there's an fMRI flatbed and a few more diagnostic machines Sam doesn't recognize. A lab tech is lying on his back on the floor, reaching up to calibrate one of them. Atop the console, a half-eaten Bird In The Bun sandwich rests in a blossom of greasy wrapping paper. Beside it towers a super-sized Global Cola.

"Hi, Ted," Dr. Pangolin says. "Remember the EEG transform we did the other day?"

He looks up. "Sure."

"Mr. Crane here has volunteered to give it a try."

Looking somewhat surprised, Ted nods and rises. "I'll make the patches. What room is the feed coming from?"

"305."

He disappears through a door at the far end of the control room. A minute passes in silence.

Sam starts to worry. "Is this standard practice?" he asks.

"No, but it's completely safe."

Unconvinced, Sam folds his arms. "What's going on?"

"How do you mean?"

"I mean, I don't think a doctor has ever spent more than five minutes with me before, much less invited me to play around on the machinery. I find this all very…unusual."

Dr. Pangolin smiles. "It's not every day we get a chance to entertain a friend of Mr. Cayman's."

"Who told you that I knew him?" he asks bemusedly.

"Dr. Dunnart."

"And what did he say?"

"Just that Mr. Cayman wanted to make sure you and your daughter were taken care of."

"Those were his exact words?"

Dr. Pangolin pauses for a moment. "As near as I can recall."

Sam takes a step toward her. "I want to see Dr. Dunnart."

Dr. Pangolin steps back. "Mr. Crane, there's no need—"

"Stop. Take me to him."

"He's at a conference in Miami."

"Call Cayman, then."

"Mr. Crane," Dr. Pangolin protests, "I don't appreciate being bullied."

"Get over it," Sam snaps. "That's what happens when you play games with my kid."

Dr. Pangolin looks dismayed. "What are you talking about?"

"I'm not Cayman's friend. I've never met the man. But he got my daughter into this drug trial. And now he's saying we're old pals and is pushing to get me into a brain scanner? Does that sound odd to you?"

"I guess."

"It's less so when you know that I'm investigating the death of Xian Mako. Does that name ring a bell?"

"I met him briefly."

"I think that Cayman is involved somehow. And if he is, it fits that he'd want a hold over me."

"Mr. Crane—"

"If there's anyone being bullied here, it's me," Sam insists. "It's an implied threat. That's why we need to have a few words. Will you help me?"

With an exaggerated sigh, Dr. Pangolin relents. "Alright, I'll give it a try." She summons her agent and places the call.

After a brief delay, Cayman's agent answers, then queries her employer. The ambient sound of an outdoor location can suddenly be heard.

"Harris Cayman here. What can I do for you, Doctor?"

"I'm here with Sam Crane, the father of one of the kids in the Lucidan trial."

A laugh. "Hello, Sam. A pleasure to meet you."

"Likewise."

"I take it you're the one who wants to chat?"

"The doctor is just running the switchboard."

"Well, I'm engaged at the moment, but I have some time tomorrow. Have you been to Havanaland before?"

"No."

"What fun. You'll have a ball. I'll send my jet to fetch you. Be at home by five today."

It takes a moment for Sam to respond. The opportunity to question Cayman in person might not present itself again. "Okay," he says finally. "What about Fiona?"

"I'm sure Dr. Pangolin and her staff will take good care of her. And I won't detain you for long. Fair enough?"

"Sure. I'll be ready."

"Splendid. Ciao."

Dr. Pangolin's agent announces the termination of the call.

"Thanks," Sam says, unsettled by the encounter.

Dr. Pangolin nods. "I hope things work out for you."

"Just take care of Fiona," he says. Without waiting for a reply, he retraces his steps to his daughter's room. He knows he should feel grateful that his daughter is in a private research hospital. It's a lot cleaner and quieter, to be sure. But it feels like he has a gun to his head.

Fiona has settled down somewhat. Dr. Jird is still there, monitoring her on his handheld tablet. "Back so soon?"

"I'd like a minute alone with her," Sam says.

"Of course," Dr. Jird says with practiced deference. "Take as much time as you need. I'll be back shortly." He steps out.

The family photos Sam loaded into the wall display dissolve from one to the next: Fiona in silhouette, a plastic pail in hand, entranced by the sun sinking into the sea; Sandra buried in sand, much to the amusement of a gleeful little girl.

His late wife. Not late—absent. There's a difference. Her face is a hammer in his head. He commands Marilyn to license some landscapes as temporary replacements. There are never any people in stock landscapes—a fact that goes a long way toward explaining their appeal.

Sam touches Fiona on the forehead, though fever isn't really a concern. What began as a diagnostic act now serves as an expression of affection. He notices her nails have been trimmed since yesterday. That speaks well of the Zvista staff.

Leaning over to whisper in her ear, he tells his daughter that he may be away for a few days. Someone will stop by, he says, without knowing who it will be. His mother-in-law perhaps, or maybe Tony. A kiss on the cheek seals the deal. Her skin smells medicinal, like the antiseptic used to wash the bedridden.

From the parking lot, Sam watches the fog muster behind Twin Peaks. In a few hours, the mist will occupy the city. It's entrancing, the stately pace of the white waves; everything else moves so fast, in jump cuts and frames per second. His reverie is ended by the Dopplered roar of a low-flying air taxi.

"Is everything alright, Sam?" Marilyn asks.

Pondering the question, Sam is almost ready to believe it was born of compassion. But he knows better. He knows that's the network's way of asking if he has any needs that can be met with a quick debit or two. For every void in your soul, there's a shrink-wrapped product to make you whole. Still, even counterfeit concern is welcome. Like a placebo, it has some effect.

"Yeah, I'm fine," he answers. "Just thinking about Fiona." He mounts his motorcycle without knowing where he's going. In four hours, he has to be home. He owes a visit to Ikura Industries, the fish distributor Ernesto mentioned. But he'd rather go early, when the boats return with their catch.

"Perhaps she'd like some art in her room," Marilyn suggests.

That's who he needs to see: Cayman's daughter. She might be able to offer some insight regarding her father.

Marilyn continues, "For a limited time, Corbis is offering its Beautiful People collection for fifty percent off. Studies indicate that clinical outcomes are seven percent better if patients are surrounded by faces as opposed to landscapes."

"Whose study?"

"Please be more specific."

"Who funded the study?"

"The International Federation of Portrait Photographers."

Sam rolls his eyes. "I'll pass, Marilyn." Over the rumble of the engine, he asks for the location of Amy Ibis.

Marilyn answers, "According to Content Corp's feed, Amy

Ibis is at the University of California, Berkeley, speaking at a demonstration."

Leaving his bike under the shade of a token tree just off Telegraph Avenue at Dwight Way, Sam makes his way toward the UC campus. Pedestrians spill from the sidewalk into the street, slowing traffic. At Moody's Liquid Pharmacy, just south of Bancroft Street, students linger over self-prescribed drinks containing unregulated herbs, hormones, and stimulants.

The UC campus is packed with protestors dressed in the clothing of the mid-1960s—not the garish hippie garb of the Summer of Love but post-Eisenhower conservative, with thin ties, bobby socks, turtlenecks, and a distinct absence of hair-care products. A few sport signs that say "Free Speech." Several hundred of these student time travelers stand in front of Sproul Hall, drunk on defiance, cheering a folk singer who's lip-synching "We Shall Overcome." Something about the scene is wrong. It takes a minute before Sam realizes what it is: no brand logos on any of the clothing or signs.

Some of the surrounding police are wearing uniforms from the same period—1964, according to the bystander who hands Sam a flyer with the headline "Why We Fight." The remaining forces of the law, loitering in the background of the reenactment, are equipped with more modern gear, like articulated body armor and microwave guns. Sam watches, fascinated, as the police of yore drag those playing protestors away. Mock scuffles unfold; pseudo-students take beatings from foam batons. It's all quite convincing, except that everyone's having a good time.

A network inquiry reveals that those present are members of the Northern California chapter of the Society for Collective Memory, a national reenactment group devoted to exploiting a loophole in decades-old legislation known as the Flag Protection Act.

Asked to elaborate, Marilyn explains that gathering to recreate a historical event represents an exception to the law, which generally limits protests to twenty people or less. Though the exemption was slipped into the statute by a Confederacy-crazed senator from North Carolina, groups beyond his constituency of Civil War buffs were quick to recognize the opportunity. So much so, in fact, that there are a number of cases before the courts in which competing historical societies are vying for exclusive performance rights to the more famous demonstrations.

"The most contentious," Marilyn says, continuing her summary of recent news coverage, "is the fight between the African-American History Project and the Aryan Foundation over the 1963 Lincoln Memorial gathering where Dr. Martin Luther King delivered his 'I Have a Dream' speech."

"Right," Sam says, more to himself than to Marilyn, "I saw something about that a few weeks ago."

"If you're interested in learning more about Dr. King," Marilyn says, "why not try a Final Days tour of Memphis? Learn what really happened when Dr. King was assassinated, with the help of a Tony Award-winning cast. You'll see Memphis through the eyes of those who were there that fateful day in April 1968. You'll visit the restored Lorraine Motel, where you'll see a reenactment of Dr. King's death. And afterwards you'll relax at the famous Peabody Hotel. Built in 1869, this historic landmark is more alive than ever with Southern hospitality. If you act now, you'll save ten percent off the Final Days weekend package rate of $12,000."

Sam doesn't answer. He's busy scanning the protestors for Amy Ibis. Pressing through the crowd, he makes his way toward the steps of Sproul Hall.

"Nice costume," jeers a youth in period dress.

Mild laughter bubbles up among the young man's friends.

Sam glares. His critic grins. Sam kicks him in the shin. He continues onward, his transgression hidden from the cameras by the crowd.

When he looks up, he recognizes Amy standing among a group of protestors under a tree. Even in costume—a knee-length white skirt, a pillbox hat, and a three-quarter-sleeve jacket—she's more beautiful than her pictures suggest. So much so that he thinks there has to be some secret deficit, a counterweight to the advantages that are hers by birth. She's staring into space, perhaps bored by the faux protest.

Sam approaches and her eyes find his. A slim scar reaches across her cheek, ever so slight, too indelible perhaps for even the best surgeons. Oddly, it pushes her closer toward perfection.

He stops in front of her, grasping for words.

"You look lost," she says, as if it's something to be desired. "It becomes you."

"I was looking for you."

"You must be Sam Crane. My father warned me about you."

Sam can't help but grin. "My bark is worse than my bite."

Her answering smile is somewhere between sultry and smirking. She tours him with her eyes. "That's a sign of remorse," she says. "The committed strike in silence."

That she's teasing him, Sam has no doubt. Whether she's being mean-spirited or playful, he's not so sure. "Is that a confession?" he asks.

"Just the truth."

"I've found that whenever someone mentions 'the truth,' that person is lying nine times out of ten."

"I painted by numbers too, when I was five. I grew out of it."

"What can I say? I'm in touch with my inner child."

Amy laughs. "Why don't you just ask me if I killed Xian?"

"That would be rude."

"A gentleman! You're more of an anachronism than these demonstrators."

"While women do tend to favor poison, there are more likely suspects. Your father, for instance."

"I suppose that's why he warned me about you." Amy appears intrigued by the possibility. "Do you really think he did it?"

"Not really, but maybe he knows who did."

A pause. Sam wishes he could read her better.

"So Xian was poisoned?" Amy asks.

"Yes. I'd have thought you'd heard."

"I don't care for the news. I find it depressing."

On cue, the demonstrators start chanting.

"I see why they banned this sort of thing," Sam observes.

"Would you like to interrogate me some place quieter?"

Sam thinks about it for a moment. "Yeah, I would."

Retracing his steps along Telegraph Avenue, Sam follows Amy to People's Park, the nearest landing area for air cars. Blasted grass and bent trees show the ravages of jet engines and fan blades. Among the 'gents who make their homes in the withered brush, most are profoundly deaf.

A black Boeing air sedan is waiting. Gull-wing doors rise in sync like Busby Berkeley cobras. Amy ducks inside; Sam follows.

"This is David, my driver," she says over the pair of idling engines.

David nods, his overbroad features shown in frightening close-up on the video monitor mounted behind his seat.

Amy sits facing forward; Sam faces backward. He is struck by how appropriate this is for someone always focused on the past.

"You don't say much," Amy remarks over the rising drone of the rotors.

"I'm the strong, silent type," Sam answers.

A cryptic smile appears on Amy's face. She looks out the window.

Berkeley recedes below. Four outboard Rolls Royce engines tilt horizontal. There's a moment of weightlessness as the air car drops just before accelerating. Out the portside window, Sam can see the missile turrets atop the Bay Bridge. The water beneath sparkles as if strewn with the ruins of a shattered sun.

Within minutes, the sedan slows over the northwestern edge of San Francisco, already buried in fog. The engines swing vertical and the craft rises for a moment as the rotors slow. Then comes a computer-calibrated drop and a gentle landing.

Sam emerges after Amy. They're standing on a landing platform. An elevated causeway connects to the beach. The platform ends at a hillside, by a lift designed to bring air cars up from street level. A stairway ascends to Sea Cliff, perhaps the city's most exclusive neighborhood. Houses in the area routinely top three hundred million. And that's for a fixer-upper.

"When you're ready to go, David will take you home," Amy says as she starts up the stairway.

Sam reminds her that his motorcycle is still in Berkeley.

"David," she says as if addressing her network agent. "Please see that Sam's motorcycle gets airlifted to his house."

Sam has Marilyn set up a temporary access code to disarm his bike's motion alarm. By the time the arrangements are made, they've reached Amy's house.

Amy leads the way through the iron gate. The front yard is small but manicured. The house is Tudor in style, built in 1932, Amy says. Vines drape its rough brick walls.

Sam is impressed. "It's lovely," he says, following Amy inside.

"Everything in its right place," she answers.

"Pardon?"

"That's how my father used to encourage me to clean up. He likes things to look a certain way."

"You sound bitter."

"I was trying for weary."

A pause.

"I'm listening."

"I know," Amy answers. "That's why I'm considering my words carefully. It's just tiresome. Everything is his."

"I can see that." Sam surveys the foyer. There's a gilt-framed mirror, its reflective silver flecked with imperfections. Overhead, a chandelier gleams. Fresh irises, perhaps a dozen, stand splayed in a vase on a marble-topped side table. Busy fleur-de-lys wallpaper reaches from the waist-high wood molding to the picture rail just above the door frames. Against the far wall, flanked by two Louis Vuitton suitcases, a grandfather clock tells time as if meting out scoldings.

"So why not live on your own? You're hardly strapped for cash."

"Now it's your turn to sound bitter." Amy turns and walks through the parlor toward the kitchen.

"I suppose I am," Sam admits, following behind. Though he's watching the shift of her hips, he adds, "You have some nice antiques."

"Thank you."

"Did you get them from Kenneth Wren?"

Amy stops in the dining room, at the kitchen door. In the muted light, she looks somewhat surprised. "Several of them. Do you know Kenneth?"

"We met."

"Does that mean you were lovers?"

Sam is surprised by the question. "Hardly." He's tempted to protest that he's straight, but decides she's baiting him. "Is that all it takes? A meeting?"

"If you're reckless."

"Sound like anyone you know?"

"I'll have to think about it."

There's something sadistic about Amy's smile. Or perhaps it's just that she seems to know how much he wants her.

"Can I get you something to drink?" she asks.

"Water would be great." Sam finds it curious that there's no help, particularly given the immaculate state of the house. Perhaps the cook is out shopping.

Amy fills two glasses with sterile water from the autoclave; she hands one to Sam and leads the way back to the dining room, then out to the balcony.

It's cold outside in the fog. The view would be spectacular in better weather. Amy takes a seat in one of the two deck chairs; Sam remains standing.

"You may want to sit down," she suggests.

Music suddenly fills Sam's head; vibrations course through his teeth.

Are you prepared for the unexpected?

How'll you fare when a bomb's detected?

Time to get your ducks in a row.

Explosions happen, don't ya know.

So insure your life with Annabel Lee!

Peace of mind will set you free.

"Damn it, I'm being streamed," he shouts over a sound only he can hear.

Amy takes his hand and pulls him down to sit on the chair beside her. The music stops.

"There's a resonator that sweeps this neighborhood," she explains. "It can only track down to shoulder-level when you're standing. Below that, it's blocked by the rooftops."

Incredulous, Sam says, "This is a residential area."

"My father thinks it was installed as a prank by one of his company's competitors." Amy runs her hands through her hair. "It's only been up a week. I've already filed a complaint, but the zoning inspectors are backlogged for months."

"I hate advertising."

"We have something in common."

A hesitant smile unfolds on Sam's face. He stares into Amy's eyes, and she, back into his. It's the coldness in her voice that makes him unsure.

"You hate advertising, but you don't mind the income," Sam ventures.

"I've been supporting myself since I was eighteen," Amy insists. "He'll buy things for me sometimes. But I make my own way. That's why I took Ibis as my surname."

"I'm impressed." Sam says nothing about the doors opened by her connections. He's exploring, not conducting a trial.

"In answer to your question: I used to have a studio south of Market. But it just sold. So I've been staying here. I'm leaving soon, through."

"I noticed the bags in the front hall. Yours?"

"Yes."

"How soon is 'soon'?"

"Tonight. I'm booked on Cayman Air too."

"So…you were expecting me in Berkeley?"

Amy's face breaks into a sly grin. "I was told you'd be accompanying me this evening," she confesses. "But I didn't expect to meet you so soon. When you showed up, I thought I'd get to know something about my traveling companion."

Sam shakes his head in mock distress. "So it had nothing to do with the pheromones in my aftershave?"

Amy laughs and beckons him over. "Come here."

Sam slips off his chair and moves to her side. She sits up and leans toward him. Her hands draw his face toward hers. The heat of her breath touches his neck. He feels angry with Nadi for no good reason.

"It's been a while since you've shaved," Amy whispers.

Then comes a kiss, cautious at first.

She undoes his belt; he, her buttons.

He knows this isn't such a good idea. But knowing doesn't mean very much.

Back in the shipping container he calls home, Sam rummages through his dresser for beachwear he knows he doesn't have. He has a habit of doing the same thing with the refrigerator: opening the door several times in succession, hoping to find food that wasn't there moments before. In a world where technology is often indistinguishable from magic, he thinks it's not such a strange superstition.

Outside, Amy is waiting in her air sedan. Their departure time has been pushed up by forty-five minutes. Sam finds that odd; a private jet ought to be able to leave at the convenience of its passengers.

In his cramped bathroom, Sam reaches into the shower to turn the water on. Through the wall speakers, a network announcer greets him. "Thank you for choosing Municipal Water—"

"Oh for chrissake!" He slams the shower stall.

"At Municipal Water, we care about the health of our customers. That's why we'd like to offer you our water security package free for three months, and for fifty dollars a month thereafter. You'll get guaranteed protection from major intestinal diseases, parasites, lead, chromium, PCB's, benzene, fecal matter, and a variety of other potential contaminants, including bacteriological agents favored by terrorists. Just say, 'Sounds good to me,' and we'll update your subscription immediately."

"Marilyn," Sam pleads, "file a complaint with the Private Utilities Commission. Use the same one I filed last month. Overwrite the date field with today's date. Also, get an installer from City Water out here as soon as possible."

"I've done as you requested," Marilyn replies. "There's an installer available on Friday at 9 a.m. with a ninety-six-hour window. Would you like to schedule the appointment?"

Exasperated, Sam leans on the wall. "So he could be here anytime between Friday and next Tuesday morning?"

"Please be more specific."

"Does the service contract guarantee that the installer will arrive during the specified window?"

"No, there is an exception for extenuating circumstances."

"How does the contract define those terms?"

"Extenuating circumstances include fire, flood, famine, war, terrorism, medical emergency, inclement weather, traffic, hunger, mood, and other obligations."

In no position to negotiate, Sam schedules the appointment and resumes his scavenging. No shower for now. He settles for a change of clothes: a fresh shirt and slacks, and out of habit, his boom suit. Boom suits are required when traveling aboard commercial airliners. Made of goat silk and pressurized foam, they're the airlines' response to terror mules. They function like flak jackets in reverse, containing any explosion from swallowed Semtex. They also serve as flotation devices and reduce the incidence of blood clots among those damned to coach seating for long periods of time.

A few minutes later, Sam emerges with an overstuffed gym bag. The roar of the engines sounds like someone is vacuuming his ears. He steps into the sedan and flops down on the seat as the gull-wing doors close, diminishing the noise. He tells Marilyn to arm his home security system.

"Let's go," Amy says to her pilot.

"What's the rush?" Sam wipes dust from his eyes.

David turns to answer as the air sedan executes an automated liftoff. Over the background noise, he explains, "Mr. Cayman's broker sent word that the FAA has scheduled an emergency press conference in forty-five minutes. It seems this is linked to increased activity at the Centers for Disease Control. The broker concludes there's a high probability that local airspace will be closed to protect against an undisclosed threat."

Sam has wanted a broker for years. They're a step up from agents, proactive rather than reactive. They are constantly bartering for, digesting, and correlating information. But as a result, they cost a fortune in database-access fees. The NSA runs the most advanced one, which analyzes domestic and foreign news and events across all media in real time; it licenses a restricted but still potent version, available by subscription to brokering systems.

Three minutes later, the sedan touches down at Pagebrin Airfield, which old-timers still call Moffett Airfield. Amy exits and Sam follows. They're at the hangar used by those who can afford their own planes, probably half a mile from the facility used by private space companies. Fifty yards west, a no-nonsense fence rises like steel hackles behind a maintenance building. To the north, a sleek Boeing 797 gets its fix of jet fuel.

Two National Guardsmen arrive in a jeep. The one in the passenger seat hops out and approaches. He's carrying a biometer to measure their hand geometry and iris patterns. After he confirms Amy's and Sam's identity, he nods curtly and jumps back in the jeep, off to screen the next passenger.

Overhead, a passenger jet climbs to cruising altitude. With a nod to David, Amy leads Sam across the tarmac to the waiting 797. Under armed guard, a crew of three is loading the plane with a substantial amount of cargo, presumably to defray operating expenses .

A liveried pilot greets them at the top of the stairs then heads past the galley toward the cockpit. The cabin smells of leather and lemon. Seats are few and far between. There's a conference table to the fore and a lounge further back. A bulkhead in the midsection prompts Sam to ask what lies beyond.

"Sleeping quarters," Amy answers.

Emerging from the galley, a flight attendant takes orders for drinks.

Almost as soon as the door descends, the plane starts to move. None of the usual flight-attendant foreplay.

Sam closes his eyes as the acceleration presses him to his seat. Opening them again, he watches as downtown San

Francisco scrolls past in the triple-paned window. The labored sound of the landing gear retracting is accompanied by a hydraulic hiss.

Above the marine layer, the sky shines perfect blue. Gazing out the window, Sam can see several relay blimps through breaks in the clouds. They look like turtles from above.

Amy is staring out the window too, lost in thought perhaps. Thirty minutes pass before Sam breaks the silence.

"Tell me about The Terrorism of Desire."

Amy swivels in her chair. "It's my current show."

"I know. But what does it mean?"

A crooked smile. "See the show."

"I will, as soon as I get back."

"You felt it this afternoon," Amy says, sipping gin on ice.

Sam nods. "I don't usually do that."

"Nor do I."

Even in the flat cabin lighting, Amy is too beautiful. Not that the lighting really matters when his mind is fogged. "The night your show opened in January," he asks, "you dined at Aquamarine with Xian Mako and your father. Was the fourth Bernard Loris from Biopt?"

A look of surprise. "How did you know?"

"Lucky guess," Sam says, quite pleased with himself. "What did you all talk about?"

"Eyeballs."

"As in blindness?"

"As in everything about them. Farming them, fixing them, and getting their gaze."

"It seems to be your father's adopted cause."

"It's self-interest," Amy says. "Advertising infects through the eyes."

"Art too."

"True enough," Amy replies, smiling. "If you ignore music."

"I do. Auto-generated pop bores me."

"Try a live show."

"I know. I should."

"Why don't you?"

"I guess I just lost touch with that scene," Sam answers, his mind still on Aquamarine. "Do you still have your log from that evening?"

Amy shakes her head. "My liability insurance requires that I keep logs no more than seven days."

"So you still have your log from Sunday night?"

"I might."

"Could I review it?"

"I'll think about it," Amy says, grinning.

Over the intercom, the pilot announces that it's now safe to move about the plane. Sam unbuckles his seatbelt, stands, and stretches.

"All four of you had fugu that night?" he asks.

"Right. I see you've been doing your homework."

"What was that about? Lack of imagination or bravado?"

Amy laughs. "Try politesse. Mako is a friend of the chef there. He insisted that we try fugu as a sign of respect."

"Was a friend of the chef."

A solemn nod.

"Was there any other reason? A celebration?"

"The opening of my show."

Sam nods, though he doesn't quite buy it. The bill went to Biopt. Presumably, the gathering had a business angle. And the absence of anyone from the museum suggests that art wasn't the primary focus of the evening.

Amy shifts in her chair. "Why do you care what went on four months ago?"

"I don't really," Sam says. "It's just that Dr. Mako had tetrodotoxin in his system. The likely source is Aquamarine."

"I think you care more than you admit."

"Fair enough. I'm trying to develop a motive."

"Any luck?"

"No. Got any ideas? Why would someone want Mako dead?"

"Are you sure he was murdered?"

"I'm not sure of anything, but it does look that way. Someone went to the trouble of dumping his body on a road after he was dead. And his corpse was defaced."

Staring out the window, Amy sips her drink. "He was a handsome man," she muses.

"Once, perhaps," Sam says, recalling the wounds. "Did you know him well?"

"We moved in different circles. He in science, me in art. My father spoke very highly of him. He dined with us a few times over the years. Very polite, always asked about other people. We talked about art mostly. He was a collector."

"Of antiques too, I hear."

Amy nods.

"Did he ever talk about galvanic spectacles?"

"All the time."

Standing behind his chair, Sam leans on the backrest. "How so?"

"Just what I said." Amy holds her sweating glass up and looks through. It distorts her eye. "He talked about them constantly. How they were used to treat everything from blindness to psychosis. He saw them as a precursor to his own work."

"An antique dealer in London said Mako bought a pair as a gift," Sam explains. "The curious thing is that the cops found them on his body."

"Why is that curious?" Amy asks.

"Well, if they were a gift…"

"Perhaps he changed his mind and decided to keep them."

Sam acknowledges the possibility with a nod. Curious that she'd propose a theory so readily. It makes him wonder. Intimacy is a kind of blindness. Has he gotten too close to see? He resolves to check his log later for unusual stress in Amy's voice.

"Could I take a look at them?"

"Unfortunately, I don't have them. I gave them to a friend and he got killed. Now they're gone."

"I'm sorry to hear that."

Sam nods. "Do you have a map to the rest room?" he asks.

Amy points toward a door near the bulkhead.

"To sustain me on my journey," he says, grabbing a handful of cashews. "It's a big plane."

"Bon voyage."

He ambles back, chewing, then brushing the salt from his hands.

The lavatory is quite spacious. On the sink, there's a selection of scented soaps and miniature cologne bottles. The linen hand towels have been folded with precision. He dabs some of the cologne on his wrist, though he's merely curious. Unlike Luis, he'd never actually use the stuff.

Refreshed, he opens the door. It comes slamming back in his face.

Sam staggers and falls, clutching his head. He can feel the door's stippled texture indented on his cheek. His left eye will be black for weeks. At least his nose isn't broken.

The door swings open. Though dazed, Sam recognizes Emil Caddis.

The Algerian is standing in the aisle, pistol in hand. "On your knees, hands behind your head," he commands.

"You—"

"Now."

An unfamiliar voice shouts something in French from the forward cabin.

Sam does his best to comply, but moving hurts. "The pilot said it was safe to move about the cabin," he says.

"He was mistaken." Emil grins. He's tall, about Sam's size. And too pretty. He could star in his own movie.

"Marilyn, alarm!"

Silence.

"She can't hear you. The relay is closed."

Sam looks for Amy, but she's not in her seat. "Where's Amy?"

"She's tied up at the moment. It's you I'm worried about."

"I'm touched." Sam rubs his sore jaw.

Emil backs up. He gestures toward the cockpit. "Not if you cooperate."

The carpet turns out to be quite easy on Sam's knees.

"Stay still," Emil commands.

When Sam sees Emil buckling himself into the nearest seat, he realizes why he's kneeling by the exterior door. He has to do something, but he's staring into the maw of Emil's gun.

"What is all this about?" Anything to buy some time.

"I had hoped you could provide some information about Dr. Mako's spectacles. But apparently not."

"You don't have them?" Sam's eyes widen.

"We're here to talk about you."

"Why's that?"

"We're a hundred seventy-five pounds over our declared weight." Emil then says to an unseen companion, "Ouvrez la porte."

That Sam understands: "Open the door."

Sam dives at Emil's feet as the door slides up into the fuselage. The sucking sound is sudden and deafening. Pressurized air explodes outward. Oxygen masks drop.

Sam's ears pop. The vacuum draft throws him against the wall. He flails, frantic. His arm catches the safety belt beneath a folded seat. His feet flap just outside the plane, like coattails caught in a car door.

The pressure equalizes, but the wind and the open door still present major problems. It's freezing. Sam again tries to stand.

"Allez!" Emil shouts through his yellow mask. He's barely audible over the roar.

Sam has no trouble hearing the gun.

The bullet strikes his chest, knocking him back. He falls, but there's nothing below him for thirty thousand feet. There's nothing to breathe, either.

His life doesn't flash before his eyes; instead, everything goes dark as his boom suit expands around him, detonated by the shell. Pressurized foam bursts from the fabric like popcorn. But getting air isn't any easier at the center of a white foam ball. Sam blacks out.

He's still falling when he comes to, but slowly. He can tell the air isn't as thin, but he can't see a damned thing. He's tumbling to earth in the style of a Mars drone, protected by polyurethane rather than a balloon. He can only imagine what he must look like from below—a downed cloud.

Though his chest hurts like hell, he starts to laugh. There isn't enough air coming through the tiny pores in his cocoon to sustain his glee for long. Still, he's feeling rather pleased with himself when he finally strikes solid ground. Only then does it occur to him that getting out might take a while.

CHAPTER SIX

"**D**ON'T MOVE," SAYS the paramedic. "We're cutting in now."

Sam squints as the setting sun strikes his face. The air is cold. "Where am I?" he asks.

"In the Sierras, a few miles south of Truckee."

Tree branches shift in the breeze. Jagged rocks resembling shark fins furrow the earth. In a clearing perhaps a hundred yards away, a helicopter sits idle.

A second paramedic guides a heat saw through Sam's foam packaging. "Feels like bread dough," he observes. Wisps of acrid smoke rise from the emitter.

"Not too close," Sam suggests.

"No worries." The second paramedic smiles reassuringly. With his reddish beard and broad frame, he looks like the sort of lumberjack that appears on maple syrup labels.

Once the foam has been cut, his partner makes a few strategic slices in Sam's shredded clothing, then offers his hand.

Sam emerges clad only in boxers. He gladly accepts a blanket.

"I'm much obliged," he says. As an afterthought, he introduces himself.

"Doug," the first paramedic replies. "That's Slevok."

"Slevok? What's that? Hungarian or something?"

"It's sponsored."

"He's a bit defensive about it," Doug says.

Slevok glares.

Sam shrugs. "What's it promoting?"

"The name comes from a character in a video game, Gazebo of Death."

"Never heard of it."

"No one has heard of it," Doug says. "It was released like twenty-five years ago."

"So it was your parents who sold your name." Sam suddenly understands. "You know those contracts expire when you turn eighteen."

"Yeah, I know. I never bothered to file for a new name. So shoot me."

"He likes it," Doug teases. "Says it's an icebreaker."

"Hey, whatever," Sam says to defuse the tension. "I'm just glad you guys found me."

Doug inspects the blood-black bruise on Sam's chest. "Looks a bit like a bull's-eye," he says. "What hit you?"

"A bullet."

"Ouch."

"Yeah. No kidding."

"And your boom suit stopped it?" he asks, nodding his head in anticipation of the answer. He pulls an anesthetic from his med kit and sprays it across Sam's chest. "I guess SilkSteel is worth the money."

Now comfortably numb, Sam feels relieved. "Well, it wouldn't do if the detonator penetrated the inner lining."

Slevok pours a bio-solvent on the foam meteorite, melting it away. "Please tell me this isn't the start of another extreme sport," he says.

Sam grins. "I wonder if I can get an endorsement out of this?"

Shouldering their gear, the two paramedics help Sam to the helicopter. All things considered, he feels pretty good.

At the Tahoe Forest Hospital, in a room built for waiting, Sam waits to be debriefed. There's an FBI agent inbound, he's told. The usual waiting room diversions make bids for his attention: manhandled magazines and a television perched at a height guaranteed to drum up business for orthopedists. The monitor is tuned to Celebrity Weather, a look at the climatic challenges facing the famously underdressed in such storied destinations as Club Med and the Hilton Islands.

Sam tries to change the channel, but his verbal commands go unanswered. He fumes. There's nothing more frustrating than being ignored by appliances. Unable to reach the manual controls, he tries to move one of the benches, but finds it's bolted to the floor.

In exchange for his blanket, the paramedics gave him an

orange jumpsuit bearing the familiar silhouette of the Yosemite oil fields. It's definitely not his color. At least it has a network interface sewn in. He asks Marilyn to acquire a new outfit for him and to have it delivered as soon as possible. "I might be mistaken for someone sentenced to community service," he complains.

To his surprise, she accepts the explanation without a keyword-based ad pitch. Something's not right. The absence of solicitations usually coincides with heavy casualties somewhere; advertisers know their copy can't compete with reality. Perhaps the war on terrorism has been renewed for another season.

Sam wanders down the hallway, past several examination rooms, to the cafeteria. The granite floor has been scrubbed raw, probably by poorly calibrated bots. A medical technician seated at one of the tables looks up from his meal and tablet for a moment.

Lining the far wall, seven vending machines offer the best of mechanical cuisine. Sam scrolls through the terms of use and liability clauses on the display screen of the leftmost machine and taps the Accept button. A shrink-wrapped vat-ham sandwich tumbles out of the illuminated cabinet's maw. He tears it open and devours it, discarding the crumpled Paranatural Farms label on the floor. This despite having agreed in his snack contract to "dispose of any brand-identifiable wrapping in such a way as to not call into question the value or quality of said product or its producer(s) or agent(s)." It's not like anyone really gets sued for abandonment of packaging; the charge only comes up after someone is nabbed for littering or some related crime.

Taking a seat, Sam asks Marilyn to stream News Tonight through the speakers in his jumpsuit. The announcer sounds hypermasculine, like a parody of John Wayne.

"…police moved quickly to control the crowd of hooligans. A department spokesman indicated that seven officers were injured in the melee before order was restored…"

"Marilyn," he asks, "what's the default filter for this stream?"

"Federal Patriot," she says as the audio fades.

"Please change it to Urban Cynic as per my preference file."

"Unable to comply. You do not have permission to overwrite government-mandated translation filters."

Sam rolls his eyes. As government-issue clothing, apparently the jumpsuit doesn't support personalization. "List authorized alternatives."

"Massachusetts Academic, Armed Texan, and Kansas Creationist."

"Set filter to Armed Texan and regenerate," Sam says without much enthusiasm for any of the choices.

Marilyn returns the volume of the stream to its former level. The announcer now has a noticeable Dallas drawl.

"Elsewhere in San Francisco, reaction to the quarantine was less violent, but just as impassioned. At City Hall, National Guardsmen carrying M50 assault rifles and Colt sidearms oversaw a spontaneous protest of the government's containment policy. Local hospitals, meanwhile, dealt with a deluge of anxious citizens, someone of whom carried guns for self-protection despite local ordinances…"

Perplexed, Sam rubs his brow. What the hell is going on? "Marilyn, stop. Summarize top news related to San Francisco in the past four hours. Sort in chronological order."

"5:45 p.m., Federal Aviation Administration closes airspace within fifty miles of San Francisco. 6:10 p.m., San Francisco quarantined; bioterrorism suspected. 6:12 p.m., Centers for Disease Control identify viral outbreak. 6:14 p.m., Governor Hutias declares state of emergency, asks for federal aid—"

"Marilyn, stop. Connect to the Zvista visitors' server. Poll Fiona's vital signs. Summarize."

"Nonessential data traffic has been deprioritized," Marilyn explains. "One moment please."

Sam just nods. He steps on his left foot with his right to keep it from tapping.

"Preferred packet routing is now available from government agencies facing budget shortfalls. Would you care to hear the pricing?"

"No, Marilyn. Just tell me if my daughter is okay."

"Her data conforms with established parameters."

Sam buries his head in his hands, relieved. "Okay. Send a voice message to the nursing staff. Begin: This is Sam Crane. I realize things may be kinda hectic around there now, but please contact me directly if the quarantine has any impact upon my daughter Fiona's care. End."

"Message sent, Sam. Based on speech analysis, the network

has determined that your call was unrelated to business. You will be billed at the social rate."

Sam spends the next few minutes trying to contact friends and acquaintances in San Francisco, but to no avail. He's in the process of hiring a crier bot to find Tony Roan and deliver a message when someone calls his name.

Dr. Stephen Ursa is approaching from across the room. Agent Gibbon is with him, though his body language suggests the two don't know one another.

"What's going on?" Sam demands.

Stephen beckons, leading the way to a vacant examination room. He shuts the door. "Was Caddis on board?" he asks.

"Yes," Sam replies. "But before I say anything, I want to know what's happening. I haven't been able to reach anyone."

Stephen leans on the papered examination bed and considers his reply. "San Francisco was hit with a biological attack two hours ago," he says finally. "An engineered virus was used. Preliminary tests indicate that the virus attacks the optic nerve. But it's still too early to determine the full impact."

"It was serious enough for you to leave town," quips Sam.

Stephen glares.

"Sorry, that was out of line," Sam says, chastened.

"Direction of this investigation has been moved up the chain," Ursa explains. "I was ordered here to determine the extent of your involvement, given that the plane you were on seems to have been the dispersal method for the virus."

Sam blinks. "Cayman's plane?"

Stephen nods. "It was ditched in the desert shortly after you made your exit."

The phrasing draws a chuckle from Gibbon.

"Made my exit?" Sam says. "Caddis was trying to kill me."

With a gesture from Stephen, Sam recounts his actions since the two last spoke. After some back and forth about his relationship with Amy, he describes the takeoff—and the unusual amount of mist he noticed trailing the plane.

At this, Stephen just shakes his head.

"There was a story a couple days ago about an outbreak in Brazil," Sam ventures. "Related?"

"We think Brazil was a trial run. We're still waiting on CDC confirmation. But we expect people to become symptomatic by tomorrow morning."

"Meaning they'll go blind?"

Stephen nods, lips tight. "Well, most of them," he says after a moment. "Based on the numbers reported in Brazil, three in ten should either be immune or lucky."

"I guess I should've bought stock in Automated Sciences when I had the chance."

A quizzical look from the two agents prompts Sam to add, "A company that makes eye-repair equipment."

Dr. Ursa gestures to Agent Gibbon and the two huddle to converse for a moment. Sam looks at the acoustic foam panels on the ceiling.

"Mr. Crane, before Emil Caddis tried to kill you, did he say anything?"

"Please be more specific," Sam says, intentionally echoing the network's vernacular.

"It doesn't make sense that you two would both be on that plane by coincidence."

"Accidents never happen in a perfect world," Sam recites.

The two FBI agents appear puzzled by the assertion.

"I agree, it doesn't make sense," he adds, replaying the events in his head.

"Dazzle us with a theory," Gibbon suggests.

"He wanted to kidnap Amy Ibis and I was in the wrong place at the wrong time."

"You're contradicting your last theory," Stephen points out. "I don't believe you were on that plane by accident either. So why?"

Sam had been hoping to keep from mentioning Mako's glasses, but it seems futile. "Well," he admits, "Caddis did want to know about a pair of antique glasses. Come to think of it, I discussed them with Amy too."

"Glasses?" Stephen asks. "What did Caddis say?"

"Right before he tried to put me off the plane, he asked if I knew where they were, which is strange because I thought he had them."

"You've lost me."

"Is there somewhere we can get a drink around here?" Sam asks. "This may take some explaining."

Reclining in his motel room, all polyester and plastic, Sam tries to relax in his newly delivered clothes—a T-shirt and chinos. The images on TV make it difficult. Both the Entertainment Channel and the News Channel are broadcasting live from San Francisco. Panic has already set in. At the entrance to the Bay Bridge, people press toward the National Guard blockade, only to be repulsed by water cannons and people-heaters.

The scene is echoed at the Golden Gate Bridge. From airborne news drones come shots of roadblocks along Highways 101 and 280. Military vessels stalk the bay. Crowds seeking relief from fear have gathered at local hospitals. Scores of aircraft rain searchlights down on a city that will see nothing but darkness by dawn.

Sam wants to get back to see Fiona, despite having been told that's not possible at the moment. He feels certain Dr. Ursa could arrange it. He resolves to raise the issue again in the morning before Ursa departs.

He's beginning to regret recounting his investigation into the death of Xian Mako. For showing his hand, all he got was a vague promise of assistance. He knows how it goes. Sources get drunk dry and discarded. The Feds don't give a damn about Mako and they want to catch Caddis on their own. Don't call us, we'll call you.

Sam rises to rifle the minibar and flops back down on the bed gripping a child-sized bottle of gin. Toying with it seems somehow appropriate, given its diminutiveness. He holds it up to his eye, enjoying the sensation of cold. Though the glass, televised light flickers, bent but beautiful.

That's how he'd describe Amy: bent but no less beautiful. Thinking about her makes him smile. Not good, he tells himself. Then he remembers wanting to run a voice-stress check on their conversation.

"Marilyn," he asks, "cue my audio log to 6:00 p.m. Identify Amy Ibis. Scan for voice stress through—"

"There is no data between 5:12 p.m. and 7:43 p.m.," she interrupts.

The interval corresponds to the time when Sam boarded the plane to the moment when the paramedics gave him the jumpsuit. Then he remembers: Caddis said the relay was closed.

"Marilyn, cue my audio log to 3:00 p.m. Identify Amy Ibis. Scan voice stress through 5:11 p.m. Flag irregular patterns for review."

"Working," she says. A few seconds later, she announces that she's done.

"And?"

"Please be more specific."

"Report results of voice stress scan."

"No irregular patterns found."

Either she's uncommonly honest or she's on something. "Marilyn, compare scan to reference scans and report closest match."

"Ninety-three percent match: Demendicil-user profile." She adds, "Discretion is the best medicine. At International Chemical, that's what we believe. And with Demendicil, you can keep your thoughts to yourself. One tablet daily protects against voice-stress scans, polygraph tests, crypto-encephalograms, and body-language translation. Give yourself the privacy you deserve with Demendicil. "

Marilyn's voice drops to a whisper and her pace accelerates. "Must have federal security clearance to purchase. Side effects may include dizziness, sleeplessness, loss of appetite, violent rages, depression, mild catatonia, hallucination, agoraphobia, nasal bleeding, uncontrollable hiccups, disregard for patriotism, subversive frugality, and empathy toward strangers."

Sam closes his eyes.

"Side effects occurred in less than one percent of test subjects. Among paid test subjects, the incidence of side effects was even less. In the unlikely event of adverse reaction, International Chemical reserves the right to access any and all personal files, records, or receipts to determine the extent of your responsibility for your condition…"

A knock on the door raises Sam's eyelids to half-mast.

"Mr. Crane?" The voice is unfamiliar.

Rubbing his face, Sam swings his feet onto the carpet then plods over the door, still dressed. His chest hurts again, now that the anesthetic has worn off.

Another knock, more urgent.

"What?" he says through the door. "Who is it?"

"Mr. Cayman wants a word."

Sam fumbles with the chain lock, then opens the door.

Two large men in white suits and tanned skin stand side by side in the corridor. Both have mustaches. One wears a pink tie and a pinkie ring tight as a tourniquet. The other wears his collar open, revealing a gold cross half-buried in chest hair.

Sam has to laugh. "You two would be the muscle."

The two men nod. "Mr. Cayman sent us to collect you," says the one with the tie. "He said you'd know what this is about."

"Do I have a choice?"

"Of course," says the man with the tie.

His companion frowns.

"You think not, Mr. Civet?" asks the man with the tie.

Mr. Civet folds his arms and shakes his head.

"May we have a moment, please?"

Sam nods. "Take your time," he says, then heads back to put his shoes on. When he returns to the doorway, it seems the two men have come to an agreement.

"All set?" Sam asks.

"Indeed," says the man with the tie. "Mr. Civet was under the impression that you didn't really have a choice because even if you declined our invitation, you'd still end up accompanying us. I have convinced him that even if one of your two courses of action might have had deleterious effects upon your person, it's still a legitimate choice. That's what makes America great: freedom."

Mr. Civet nods solemnly.

"Well, I'm anxious to meet with Mr. Cayman," Sam says, "so lead on. Mind if I let my friends know I'm leaving?"

The man with the tie summons a genial smile. "If you're referring to the two FBI agents in the rooms across the hall, I think it best that you let them sleep. The mountain air can be most intoxicating. If I had to guess, I'd say they'll be asleep most of the day. Don't you think, Mr. Civet?"

Mr. Civet purses his lips and nods. Sam notices that the "Sominal Says Do Not Disturb" signs have been hung outside the agents' rooms.

The man with the tie gestures down the corridor. "After you, Mr. Crane."

By six a.m., Sam is airborne again. Cayman's plane is smaller this time, a Gulfstream Ten. It's still quite comfortable. The man with the tie—Mr. Fossa, Sam has learned—is playing cards with Mr. Civet. They tell him none of the network's various electronic diversions are available; the relay transmitter has been closed on Cayman's orders. Sam is more than a bit annoyed, given the goings-on at home. He needs to talk to quite a few people.

His only entertainment during the five-hour flight to Havanaland is a selection of movies cached during previous trips. He scrolls through the files on his seat's video system. He's seen most of the action titles: The President, Revenge of the President, and The President Strikes Again. He's heard good things about The President and the Despot, but he's not in the mood for a saccharine buddy picture. He settles for The Importance of Being Rich, a comedy of manners and mix-ups supposedly based on a true story. Anything to take his mind off terrorism.

Somewhere over Arkansas, videoed out and gorged on pretzels, Sam returns to the puzzle in his mind. If Caddis killed Jacob, why doesn't Caddis have the glasses? Because Jacob sold them before Caddis killed him? Or because someone else killed him and took them before Caddis got there? And if the glasses were so important, why were they left in plain sight, undamaged, on Mako's beaten corpse? It only makes sense if Mako's killer was unaware of their significance. Or if the glasses meant something different to Mako's killer than to Caddis. Then there's Cayman. And Amy. And the apparent absence of typical forensic evidence—nothing captured on video, no useful DNA, fingerprints, anything.

Sam bangs his head against the Plexiglas inner window, eliciting curious glances from his two traveling companions.

"A penny for your thoughts, Mr. Crane," says Fossa.

"They're hardly worth that," Sam grumbles.

"Such low self-esteem." Fossa shakes his head.

"You don't approve?"

"You should look into Dr. Trey-Pak Bat. Technology, Emasculation, and Post-Modern Self-Realization. His lectures changed my life. I've been a subscriber for five years now."

"How much have you paid the good doctor in that time?"

Fossa's brow furrows, reflecting some mental gymnastics. "It's not about the money," he contends. "It's about mastering our inner machines."

"And that's priceless," Sam deadpans.

"You get what you pay for," Fossa retorts. "Isn't that right, Mr. Civet?"

After mulling the question, Mr. Civet nods.

Fossa continues, "Dr. Bat has a name for people like you—"

"Here comes the jargon—"

"Syphons. Your insecurities drain the people around you."

"What does he call draining the wallets of the gullible?"

Fossa shakes his head, evidently disappointed. "You're not much of a detective, are you?"

Sam turns toward the window, but can't let the comment go. "Technically, I'm a spec," he counters, unwilling to concede the point. "I pursue cases that I choose."

"An information speculator. A detective. Call it what you

will. Yet you look away from the truth. Is it because you can't see within or you do not wish to?"

Sam sneers. "Such musings from the muscle. Who'd have thought?"

Fossa looks startled. "I see I've touched a nerve."

Mr. Civet smirks. Fossa turns his attention back to the card game. Sam's gaze wanders among the clouds below.

A moment later, Civet laughs exultantly. "Gin!"

Shortly after two p.m., the plane lands in Havanaland. Meticulously restored to its pre-Castro glory, the resort island is now managed by the Leisure Group, a division of Content Corp. As the Ministry of Tourism's recent ad campaign proclaims, "Imagine Williamsburg with low necklines, bare midriffs, and high stakes. That's Havanaland. More fun than the Puritans ever had."

The air on the tarmac is stifling. Through the humid heat, the passenger terminal shimmers as if shown on a faulty screen.

At the urging of Fossa and Civet, Sam descends from the plane to board an olive-drab jeep idling on the asphalt. Sam asks whether it's a replica.

Voice raised above the drone of jet engines, the driver says that it's authentic. "From the Korean War," he insists. "Mr. Cayman collects military vehicles."

The four men head toward the city center on the elevated toll expressway. Traffic is sparse; it's like living a commercial. The open road conveys a sense of freedom, possibilities, and progress—except for the rickety jeep. On the public road below, cars crawl.

A few minutes later, tires crackle through gravel in the courtyard of the old monastery Cayman has converted to a villa. The grace of its Georgian architecture remains undimmed, even darkened by years of exhaust. Two Cuban laborers are in the midst of loading protective cases into a commercial truck. A handful of other crates and boxes stand stacked on the stones. A radar dish spins at a leisurely pace atop an SUV.

Sam follows Fossa and Civet inside past two guards armed with carbines. Portraits of conquistadors line the walls of the expansive foyer. A baroque chandelier beckons the eyes upward. The place could be a museum but for the absence of a gift shop.

Beside the door leading outside, there's one work that seems out of place: a child's scribble. Scrawled on cheap, yellowing paper, it rests on an acid-free mat in an ornate gilt frame, under glass. Seeing it, Sam feels guilty that he has similar drawings stuffed in storage somewhere.

"Mr. Cayman awaits, on the terrace," says Fossa, gesturing toward the doors at the far side of the chamber. "And just so you know, you're off-network here."

"Looks like you're moving house," Sam observes as he traverses the foyer and exits though the double doors.

Fossa offers no reply.

The terrace overlooks the sea, today pristine blue under the cloudless sky. Harris Cayman stands watching the waves, hands clasped behind his back. He's taller than Sam expected. He wears a white suit, and a white hat with a black band on his graying head. To the right, under an umbrella, a table has been set with two chairs and china. Cold water in a carafe, clouded by condensation, resembles mercury though the glass. In the sun, the silverware shines gold.

"What is it you want, Mr. Crane?"

"Answers."

Cayman laughs. "I have questions. Will you indulge me?"

"Sure."

For a moment, Cayman remains silent, still transfixed by the sea. Sensing movement, Sam glances at the garden to the right. A flash of light catches his eye. It's the scope on a guard's rifle. From his post in the bushes, the guard stares back.

"Your security doesn't make me feel secure," Sam observes.

"A necessary rudeness these days, I'm afraid. Try not to think about it."

"Ignorance is bliss, eh?"

"A sentiment too often lacking in detectives."

Cayman turns. He's a handsome man, the sort always pictured with women half his age in ads for Italian suits, Swiss watches, or German cars. In the tropical climate, his pale skin screams fraud.

"I consider myself a spec," Sam says.

"So you said to Mr. Fossa. Is that your reflexive response?"

Sam shrugs. "Were you riding remote the whole time?"

"You're a seeker of truth. Fair enough?"

Sam musters half a smile. "I'll try to remember that next time I'm head-down in a dumpster."

Cayman gestures toward the table and takes a seat. Sam does the same.

"There's no shame in that," Cayman insists. "Most are not. Most prefer to be lied to."

"I suppose that makes it easier to get ahead in advertising."

Cayman grins. "Yes, you do see, don't you? You have the sight."

"And you? A seller of lies?"

Cayman lifts the carafe and pours two tall glasses of water. Far above, a jet contrail scars the sky.

"I'm an evangelist, Mr. Crane. A merchant of happiness, of forgiveness and indulgence. And there's no shame in that either. The world needs both you and me. Of course, you're not always welcome. And that's what we need to discuss."

Sam shrugs. "Popularity is your concern. Let's talk about my daughter."

"You still haven't answered my question. What do you want? Not on a superficial level, not on a professional level, but deep down, what do you want most of all?"

"For that waiter over there to bring lunch."

Cayman gestures toward the waiter, who nods and ducks into the house. "Come now, Mr. Crane. Surely you can do better. What do you really want?"

"For you to get to the point?"

Cayman looks disappointed. "Not to see your daughter awaken? Not to hold your wife in your arms again? The truth, Mr. Crane. Or does it hurt too much?"

It does. Sam stands and hurls his glass to the ground at Cayman's feet. It shatters, splintering bright in the sun. There's movement in the garden. Cayman stands too, hand held out toward the bodyguard.

"Yes, it goddamn hurts!" Sam growls.

Cayman opens his arms. "There. You call down God's damnation because you long for his power. And who wouldn't want to be God? Who would abjure comfort, security, bliss?"

"I wasn't aware that Heaven's hiring."

A young man in a suit emerges from the house with a broom and dustpan to gather the broken glass. Sam follows Cayman away from the table so as not to interfere.

"My point is that we're all would-be gods," Cayman says. "The way we express that will to power varies, but our purpose remains the same—we're planning, each and all, a coup against Fate. Deep down, we're all dictators."

Sam shrugs. "So?"

"What would you do for that kind of power?"

There's something in Cayman's voice, a curious fervor. It's disturbing. Sam can only laugh.

Cayman laughs too. "I don't mean to sound delusional," he insists. "But this is big."

"Are you going to tell me what the hell you're talking about?"

"In due time, Mr. Crane."

"I'm not a patient man."

"Your daughter is a patient at Zvista. Perhaps you can learn from her example."

"Is that a threat?" Sam demands.

"It's a statement of fact. Is the truth threatening?"

Sam's eyes narrow. His fists tighten.

"Come, sit down," Cayman says with a shrug. "Lunch is served."

Sam turns to find the table set and the terrace swept, with the waiter in full retreat toward the house. For the second time, the two men sit down. On serving platters sit a Niçoise salad, a sliced baguette, and a wedge of cheese already losing form in the heat.

"You're right, of course, about your daughter," Cayman says. "She is my hostage. But before you go reaching for my throat, allow me to explain."

Sam relaxes his grip on his butter knife, despite being confident that he could drive the blunt blade through Cayman's neck before the bodyguards could react. He knows it would be a stupid move. Score one for impulse control.

"You were supposed give up on Dr. Mako," Cayman says, hands pressed together as if in prayer. "Why didn't you?"

"I was supposed to take a fall? That's how Luis put it."

"Indeed. Sadly, you're more competent than Luis indicated."

"So, did you have Mako killed?"

"No, actually."

"How about you make my life easier and tell me who did?"

Cayman shakes his head. "I can't help you there."

"Can't or won't?"

For once, Cayman is silent.

"Why involve me at all?"

"Local police franchises have reporting requirements that specs don't have to observe," Cayman explains. "Farming cases out means certain details don't make it into the federal databases in a timely manner. It was our hope that you'd go through the motions, get frustrated, and move on to something more likely to pay off."

"I probably would have, but for Jacob getting killed."

"For the record, I had nothing to do with that."

"Who did?"

"I'm afraid I don't know. I wish I did."

"Do you know why?" Sam asks.

"Dr. Mako's glasses, I presume," Cayman answers, reaching for some salad.

Sam serves himself too. "The question remains: Why? Why are they so important?"

"Heaven's hiring."

Sam stares at Cayman, who smiles back oddly. "Are you mentally ill?" he asks, half-serious.

Cayman's eyebrows rear and he laughs. "We all want such power. You, to protect your daughter. Me, to protect mine. Others, for other reasons. Amy and I haven't always seen eye to eye, but she's all I have. As a father, I expect you understand."

"To protect her from Emil Caddis?"

"Yes. She had a relationship with him some years back, before he took up arms. Now she's his hostage, though I'm not sure if she knows it."

"Like Fiona?"

Cayman's lips hint a heroin smile. "Such a quick study. I warned Amy about Emil, but she delights in displeasing me. It's how she works out her guilt about her wealth and mine."

"What does Caddis want?"

"The very thing you'll use to find him: Mako's glasses."

"What's so damn important about those glasses?"

"They contain the key to the kingdom."

"Can we dispense with the cryptic self-indulgence?" Sam snaps.

Cayman looks disappointed. "The word you're looking for is 'cryptographic.' But I'll show you the kingdom tomorrow."

"Why wait?"

"You look tired. It's something best seen with fresh eyes."

Sam does feel tired. Too much so. He can't find the words.

"Don't fight it. The trip's more enjoyable asleep."

Cayman's lips continue to move, but the sound fades. Looking up, the sky seems slick with Vaseline. Sam tries to rise, but descends instead. Cutlery clatters on the terrace. Facedown on the flagstone, he can see his reflection in his host's newly shined shoes, then nothing.

Sam awakens blindfolded by gauze. His eyes are burning, as if he's spent too long in a public pool. The skin on his face feels taut—like the restraints on his arms and legs. The scent of antiseptic is overwhelming.

The air here is different, desert-dry. He's hungry again, so some time has passed. He could really do with a glass of water. The uncomfortable vinyl chair in which he is reclining would be well suited to an unlicensed dental practice based in the back of a van.

"Marilyn, where am I?" he croaks.

"Your agent can't hear you here." It's a young man's voice, unfamiliar. "How are you feeling?" he asks.

"I've been better. Are you a doctor?"

"I'm just the box op."

"The what?"

"I run the Cherry Picker."

Sam tries to rise, but can't. "What the hell did you do to me?"

"I upgraded your eyes."

Sam's heart slams. "You...messed with my eyes?" He can barely form the words.

"Don't worry. You'll be able to see fine before too long. It's just about time to take the bandages off."

"You replaced my eyes!"

"Chill," says the young man. "I did you a favor. You'll see. These are special."

"Let me up," Sam says, trying to buck his restraints.

"Uh, let me get Mr. Cayman."

Footsteps recede, to be subsumed by the drone of the ventilation system. Sam waits, testing his restraints repeatedly, though certain their strength remains the same.

A few minutes later, several people enter the room. Someone loosens the leather belts. Fat fingers replace the straps and lift Sam to his feet. He resists, to no avail.

"Easy, Mr. Crane." It's Cayman's voice.

Sam is seething. "You're a dead man."

"In time," Cayman replies. "In time."

"I'm going to kill you."

"You should be on your knees thanking me. But you need to keep up."

Footsteps again, heading away.

"Come, Mr. Crane," says Fossa, squeezing Sam's right arm. "Don't struggle."

Sam guesses Civet must be the one gripping his other arm. He's led along a corridor, then up some stairs. The air starts moving again, suggesting a more open space beyond a door. Footfalls form a polyrhythm with themselves as they echo off stone walls.

"Watch your step," says Fossa.

After the threshold comes the warmth of the sun. Light too, red as seen through the blood in his eyelids—an approximation of dawn. The gauze comes off and Sam's eyes clamp tighter.

"You'll be sensitive to light for a few more hours," Cayman says. "The blurring should be just about gone."

Fossa and Civet release Sam's arms.

"What do you see?" Cayman asks.

Sam opens his eyes and a Mexican village fades into view. He's standing in the doorway of a Franciscan mission. Its neoclassical adobe façade appears untouched by the passage of time. The surrounding buildings all hew to the mission style. A short distance down the road in either direction, locals go about their daily business. Shoppers pick over the selection at a fruit stand. Others travel to and fro, some with bags in hand. Outside a bicycle shop, an elderly man is adjusting some spokes.

"Everything in its right place," Sam says, thinking of Amy.

"Indeed," Cayman answers, eyeing Sam strangely.

More notable is what's missing: There are no power lines or street lamps. No cars. No animals, despite the twitter of unseen birds. No signs. No ads. Not a scrap of trash.

"Where are we?"

"In my head," Cayman says. "That's the easiest way to describe it. More literally, you're at our main beta site south of Nogales. But rather than explain, allow me to show you." His gaze drifts up toward that ghost space occupied by agents and others without a physical presence, a place always above the ground and beyond the circle of personal space, the traditional residence of the divine. "Begin demo," he says, then glances back at Sam. "Don't worry about the sound. That'll be addressed in our next release."

Cayman and his henchmen fade from view, followed by the villagers. Sam turns in place, confused.

"We're still here," Cayman says. "Just watch."

Some of the ambient sounds drop out—the birds, distant hammering, voices. The wind remains.

The wire-frame view of a 3D modeling environment appears over the visible objects in the world. Every angle, every line of every structure glows. Then each object disappears, one by one, until nothing is visible but a grid of lines that converge at the vanishing point of the horizon. The effect is profoundly disorienting. Sam himself is the last object to vanish.

"Christ." Sam covers his face with hands he can no longer see. The lines disappear too, leaving only darkness.

A voiceover begins. "In the beginning there was nothing. Then God said, 'Let there be light.' And there was still nothing, but you could see it better."

The grid is visible once again. Sam can't quite place the voice, but he's certain it's someone famous, which counts for something.

The voiceover continues, "And as Nature abhors a vacuum, we at Synthelegy said, 'Let there be ads.'"

Sam's sight returns. The village is different: Every square inch of wall space now boasts a billboard, poster, or storefront display. There are more people than before, too, some with strategically tattooed logos, some saddled with sandwich boards. The streets now have trash, though every candy wrapper and cast-off soda bottle appears positioned for optimum brand visibility.

A Global Cola BigBuckit cup rolls by. It's actually more barrel than cup; even on its side it comes up to his knees. Sam reaches down to pick it up. His hand passes through and the cup vanishes. A coupon appears in the air, accompanied by a short trumpet blast. It's mostly transparent, but no less legible: "You've earned ten percent off your next cool, refreshing Global Cola!"

There's a second paragraph in a remarkably small font: "Some exceptions apply. Offer void where prohibited. This advertisement is in no way intended to induce consumption of Global Cola. Any such act is solely the choice of the consumer, who assumes full liability for his or her actions and their consequences including, but not limited to, gastrointestinal distress, tooth decay, fructose-induced violence, and obesity. Global Cola is not guaranteed to be cool or refreshing."

As soon as Sam finishes reading the words, the coupon fades and a colorful arrow appears. It hovers over a storefront just down the street, beneath the words "Redeem your coupon here in the next five minutes and receive a free refill (if you can handle it)!"

"Once we link up with network profiles, the ads will be much more closely tailored to your interests," Cayman explains.

Sam offers no acknowledgement. He's busy turning his head this way and that to see which graphics track with his gaze and which remain fixed on the landscape.

The voiceover resumes. "This is the world seen with Oversight, a new sensory mediation technology that allows real-time dynamic masking as well as static graphic overlays. It grants content providers the ability to overwrite any visible object, moving or still, with alternate imagery. By interfacing directly with the optic nerve, Oversight ensures uninterrupted delivery of marketing messages and quarantines customer perception from the distractions of competing ads."

An eye logo appears. The accompanying ad copy reads, "Oversight. Because seeing is buying." The logo fades.

"Rather seamless, wouldn't you say?" says Cayman. "I'll concede our audio delivery needs work. But we've had to push up the release date due to recent events. Once we upgrade the cochlear module, we'll have full surround and source placement. Next year, we hope to bring olfactory and haptic input online too. Then the illusion will be complete. In the meantime, things may sound a bit tinny."

Clutching at his temples, Sam groans. "You stuck a pair of Auglites in my head."

"Much more than that, Mr. Crane. Auglites are a novelty item. We're in the processes of litigating them away; they're based on stolen alpha code. That's why they're really only useful for overlays on fixed objects. Your eyes see so much more.

We can mask people, or any object in your field of vision, fixed or in motion. We can do it so it looks real. The light and shadows behave as they should. There are no blank spaces in revealed background surfaces. These are nontrivial technical challenges. It's regrettable that the introduction of Auglites to the market has forced us to launch earlier than we'd have liked, but there it is."

"So this is your bid to win the war for eyeballs?" Sam's voice drips with contempt. "Who's backing this? Content Corp?"

A subtle smile takes shape on Cayman's lips. "You have to ask yourself at this point, 'Who isn't?'"

"The Amish," Sam says.

Cayman laughs. "Think about it, Mr. Crane. What better way to deny the intrusions of the modern world than with new eyes? Every object that offends their sensibility can be banished from sight. Cars become horse-drawn carriages. Power lines become one with the sky. Bare midriffs become modest sackcloth. Faces can be veiled."

"At what cost?"

"None. The cost is underwritten by the many interested parties."

"I'm not talking about money." Sam stares skyward. The witch from The Wizard of Oz flies by on a bottle of Brahmin Beer.

"You're implying that there's some spiritual cost, is that it?"

"Your world sickens me."

"But it's not my world," Cayman insists. "It's yours. People see what they wish. They seek out that which corresponds to their worldview. They congregate with their own. For years, we've had news and entertainment tailored for Republicans, Democrats, Christians, Muslims, and Jews. How is this any different?"

"Not everyone is like that."

"Not everyone, I'll grant you. But such independent thinkers are statistically insignificant in the overall scheme of things. And even they have to apply some filters to their reality to avoid being overwhelmed by contradictions, by the hypocrisy and horror of it all. There's simply too much irreconcilable information. What I'm offering is a way to see clearly."

Sam struggles to find the words. "People won't stand for this," he stammers, clutching his head.

"No, they will fall to their knees and beg for it, as they do when they pray. We're talking about people who traded their privacy for the opportunity to share cat pictures with the world. You're resentful because it was forced upon you."

"As opposed to those infected in this outbreak?"

"That's not my doing," Cayman says.

Sam sneers. "Your opportunity then?"

Cayman smiles. "You've got it all wrong. We're not taking anything away. We're retrofitting reality with power steering. You'll still be welcome to watch the homeless starve while you fill your belly. But most will appreciate the option to overwrite them with a lamppost."

Fighting nausea, Sam takes long, slow breaths. His new eyes fill him with revulsion. Overhead, birds swerve in formation. Or they might be a flock of pixels tracing some equation. It's hard to tell.

Cayman pats Sam on the back. "If you're done feeling sorry for yourself, we can talk business," he says, setting off down the street. "Come."

Sam follows, with Fossa and Civet bringing up the rear. He's staring at Cayman's impossibly white jacket when the words "Sport coat by Armani, $45,000" appear. He looks away and the characters disappear. The system is tracking his eye movements. Further testing reveals there's a one-second threshold before any imposition appears.

Cayman turns right and heads through a crowd. He makes no effort to avoid those shopping at the market, but he does not collide with anyone either. They have no substance; they exist merely to augment the experience of shopping. Sam wonders if Cayman even sees them.

A moment later, it looks as if Cayman will walk into a wall. Instead, he disappears. Sam hesitates, extending his hand. He grasps at air.

"Disconnect Mr. Crane," Cayman says to his agent.

The sky fades to a less appealing shade of blue. The village disappears. In its place, there's parched earth and scrub brush. A single structure stands a stone's throw ahead. Relatively narrow, it extends several hundred yards to the west. It looks like a hydroponics facility, the sort of place that grows square tomatoes. Perhaps a dozen dust-caked vehicles bake in the sun. On the southern side, three massive pipes bridge the gap between the main building and what appears to be a pumping station.

The four men enter and pass through a security checkpoint.

They're greeted by a Honda bot in marionette mode—the operator, wearing a motion-mirroring suit, is standing in an adjacent room behind bulletproof glass. Machine mimics man as both wave everyone onward.

"Why are we here?" Sam asks.

"We're sightseeing," Cayman answers.

They pass a pair clad for the clean room. Nods are exchanged, but no words. Ahead, a pair of steel doors bears a sign warning that only authorized personnel are permitted.

Just inside is a dressing room. Cayman, Fossa, and Civet slip into bio-containment suits. Sam does likewise. The group continues through the next set of doors into a decontamination chamber. Sprinklers erupt overhead, a sudden bloom of inverted flowers. Blowers dry everyone, and then the air is still. The final set of doors open.

A steel catwalk extends into the distance. To either side stretch lap pools, perhaps twenty feet wide and hundreds long. At first glance, the two pools appear to be tiled with turquoise and alabaster. It takes a moment before Sam realizes he's looking at eyes in brine.

There are thousands, perhaps hundreds of thousands, of them, staring into the air, expectant. This batch is blue. They glitter, even in the dim light. Disembodied, they might be pale sapphires, or rows of roe from some fantastical fish. It's easier to see them so than as organs of sight.

"Breathtaking, isn't it?" Cayman asks, muffled by his bio suit.

"And you don't have to pay extra for surveillance," Sam observes.

Cayman chuckles and continues walking at a leisurely pace. Sam follows absently, mesmerized by the sea of eyes. Fossa and Civet are never far behind.

"Why bother growing tissue when you could use chips?" Sam asks.

"You're talking about retinal implants?"

"Yes. Isn't that what doctors usually use for eye problems?"

"If cost were the only issue, then yes, silicon fabrication would be the answer. Or mere contact lenses. But there's the issue of marketing. A chip in the eye is an artificial alteration. What we're offering is a natural replacement. Our focus group was far more receptive to the latter."

"So? You use chips too."

"But they're packaged in eyes. And that's what we're selling."

Some distance ahead, where an intersecting catwalk leads to doors left and right, a handful of workers in clean suits operate a dredge attached to a track in the ceiling. They're working quickly, packing the spherical harvest in coolers for transport. The floor grating glistens with the jelly of eyes crushed underfoot.

The four visitors pass them and exit through the door to the right, removing their bio suits in another decontamination chamber.

They step outside, into the shade of the building. Out in the sun, laborers are loading refrigerated trucks that bear the logo of the Safefood grocery chain—the import tax on edible goods is much lower that the tax on medical goods.

"Your ride back," Cayman says, gesturing toward the nearest semi.

"All out of private planes?"

Cayman ignores the jibe. "I want you to go home and make discreet inquiries about selling Dr. Mako's glasses," he says. "Soon thereafter, expect Emil or one of his doubles to contact you—"

"One of his doubles?"

"He has several in his employ," Cayman explains. "Now let me continue. You will say that the glasses can be found in a revolving escrow vault on the border of North and South Korea. The price is the return of my daughter. Regardless of what he says, that's the only possible deal. I have arranged for you to work through a Saudi agency, International Hostage Brokers, Ltd. With Amy and the glasses both in the vault, the exchange will be made. After that, you and your daughter are free to do as you please. You will, of course, receive some consideration for services rendered."

Sam doesn't reply immediately. He's pissed. But he can see no way out. And he's still trying to fathom the magnitude of Cayman's scheme. It must go beyond Cayman; one man doesn't redraw the global media landscape without friends in high places. What was it Ursa said? "Direction of this investigation has been moved up the chain." Could Cayman and the Feds be working together? Why? Do they just have a common enemy in Emil Caddis?

"Alright," Sam says finally. "I happen to like Amy, so I'll do what I can. But what makes you think Caddis will believe me?"

"He thought you had the glasses before," says Cayman. "Convincing him that he was right all along should be easy. That's why you must be the delivery boy."

Sam nods.

"Your biometrics have been registered for Room 451 at the X Hotel. Inside, you'll find an eyeglass case with a replica of Dr. Mako's spectacles. You're registered under the name Ryan Wolfe. Don't go home."

"What'd you do? Make a cast of my body while I slept?"

"Don't use any standard network interfaces," Cayman says, ignoring Sam's question. "You can be located if you do. We've deactivated your earpiece and the inputs in your clothing. You can issue voice commands as if you had a dentonator; your cochlear audio module will transmit them. This one also has the advantage of being able to broadcast incorrect location data. It can mask you from anyone but us when you're not using the network. Anyone searching for you can still get close when you do go online by checking router proximity and triangulating, even without the APS data, but we've got people on the ground in San Francisco with cloned chips to make that more difficult too."

"Who's going to be searching for me?"

"Caddis' people, federal agents, Sinotech spies, to name a few. If they catch you, don't mention your new eyes if you want to keep them."

Sam manages a resigned laugh. "If they're so valuable, why give them to me?"

"If you want to hide something, hide it in plain sight. And you may need those eyes if things don't work out with Emil.

Also, our visual presentation layer isn't entirely functional yet, so you may experience anomalies."

"Bugs in my head. That's just what I need."

In a semi full of eyes, Sam heads home. A Mexican named Angel is driving. He speaks English well, though not very often. That suits Sam fine; he's got plenty to talk about with others. He spends the first hour interacting with Marilyn, dealing with a message queue that's full of demands for his time or money or both. Then he checks the news.

The situation in San Francisco remains tense. Civil unrest has been fairly light, since blindness limits one's ability to protest. Travel restrictions into or out of the Bay Area continue, though Angel insists that his semi will be allowed through; some ten hours ago, President Vaca directed FEMA and the CDC to establish eye-replacement units at hospitals, malls, and Jiffy-Tuck Health Centers. The big surprise in all the chaos: Content Corp and Entertainment Corp are setting aside differences and ordering out-of-town employees to volunteer as guides and personal shopping assistants (with, Sam suspects, a particular eye for the products of major ad buyers). A few suspiciously telegenic company executives have even gotten in on the act. By chance, cameras happened to be present and rolling at the time.

To bring his life-to-advertising ratio back into compliance with his network contract, Sam then sits through seventy minutes of commercials on the passenger-side heads-up display. At one point, bored by a testimonial for yet another recreational shopping drug—"I used to suffer from buyer's remorse, but ever since I started taking Perchaset…"—Sam focuses on the scrolling landscape beyond the window projection, dull desert brown though it is. He's startled when the luminous image of the now-happy shopper shifts back toward sharpness to match the focus of his eyes. Whether this is a function of his new eyes or an upgraded attention-monitoring system in the semi's interface, he can't say. But it's really annoying.

Finally they reach Nogales. Broken windows and broken pavement scar the city and its suburbs. The Free Trade Zone factories known as maquiladoras stand mostly abandoned now that the jobs flowing southward have dried up. Cheap structures of corrugated steel served well when leveraging cheap labor. But motion-mirroring and automation changed that equation. A thousand bots slaved to a single master craftsman make more for less than a human assembly line. Such systems require different infrastructure—uninterrupted power, temperature control, engineering support, and high security. All of which can be had north of the border, or anywhere else with wealth enough to afford the initial investment. Now only fences remain, dividing and subdividing without anything to protect.

Sam descends from the cab at a Titters truck stop just beyond the U.S. border crossing, leaving Angel to get approval for his freeway route plan with the Homeland Defense Office travel registrar on site. The family-friendly casino-diner-strip club has been built to echo the design of the Titters logo—two bulging orbs with detailing depicting either pupils or areolas atop a faint Cheshire-cat grin. Its two joined domes pose an anatomical Rorschach test for patrons and a conundrum for indignant litigants who've tried for years to bring obscenity charges against the owners.

As at all Titters franchises, the décor is an incongruous mix of lowbrow, low cut, and low country. The neo-Dutch diner's proximity to Mexico is apparent only in the soccer games on the wall-mounted video screens and in a few Spanish-sounding menu options. Perhaps a dozen drivers mill about, some pumping one-armed bandits, others chatting at the bar or perusing the porn in the Titters gift shop. Hofbrau barmaids shout orders to the kitchen, flagrantly flouting dietary privacy regulations. However, the likelihood of being reported to one's insurer is somewhat low, given that a snitch would face the stigma of having visited a Titters in the first place.

Famished, Sam orders a Titters Virgin Rookworst, which is twice the price of the unbranded alternative, but comes with a certification of genetic purity that also guarantees of the absence of lead, chromium, benzene, and other contaminants. Such toxins aren't usually present in generic sausages either, but Titters puts its promise in writing.

He asks for a beer.

The waitress, sporting surgical cleavage that would require the guidance of a sherpa, asks, "What size? We have Sissy, Puny, and Massief."

"Four Massiefs for Table Five," bellows a nearby barmaid.

A glance at the other tables reveals that other diners have made the same choice. "Has anyone actually ever ordered a Sissy beer?" Sam asks.

The waitress smirks.

SAM LOGS INTO the Zvista site to check on Fiona while he eats. She looks peaceful. Moments after he tells Marilyn he's available for messaging, she alerts him to an incoming call from Luis. The dapper policeman's face flickers into view.

"What the hell are you doing down in Arizona?" he demands.

"Following a lead. Things a bit crazy up there?"

Luis nods wearily. "You could say that. More than half my guys caught the bug. I got lucky."

"Is there anyone left to admire your suits?"

"Seriously, Sam. This is bad."

"Cheer up. I'm hitching home in a truckload of eyes."

An eyebrow rises, furrowing Luis' forehead.

"The FEMA folks will be able to tell you how they'll be allocated," Sam continues. "Have your people start lining up now."

"Thanks. I'll do that."

"So what was it you wanted to say?"

Luis glances off-camera for a moment, as if the words he's trying to find have taken to buzzing around his head.

"What?" Sam asks. "Lose your teleprompter?"

"You're off the Mako case."

"Tell me you're joking, Luis."

"Sorry, Sam."

"You gave that case to me!"

"And now it belongs to the Solve-O-Matic."

Sam slumps back in the banquet, sliding down the vinyl, and stares at the ceiling.

"We'll work something out compensation-wise when things calm down," Luis continues.

"You collar someone?" Sam asks, incredulous.

"As a matter of fact, yes."

"Come on, Luis. Who got fingered? I want to be blown away by the machine's deductive powers."

"A 'gent named George Gannet. We picked him up this morning."

"I want to look at the audit log."

"Such hatred for our poor little machine," Luis marvels.

"The Solve-O-Matic solves budget problems, not crimes," Sam snaps. "You know that as well as I do."

"Look at the stats, Sam. It has a sixty-five percent clearance rate. That's better than eight out of ten of the specs I use regularly. That's better than you did last year."

"It's been a bad year or two," Sam admits, "but your stats are crap. You've been tossing the machine softballs and giving your people stone-cold whodunits."

"It worked with the easy cases. Now it's doing the same with the harder ones. What do you want me to say?"

"You'll think of something when it comes for your job."

"I'm management, Sam."

Sam exhales, as if the weight of his hate was compressing his chest. "I should be back in town in the morning."

"I'll look for you then."

CHAPTER SEVEN

ON SILENT STREETS, hydraulics wail and hiss. Commuter vehicles usually drown the sound, but the sightless are staying off the roads today. A garbage truck screeches, rumbling to a halt beside a pile of refuse scattered across a storefront. In entrails and cellophane, the Homeless Union has sent a message. Waiting on the curb with cash-in-hand penitence, the store's frazzled owner now knows better than to chase 'gents from his front steps. In all likelihood, the garbage men on the truck were the ones who delivered the mess in the first place.

Sam finds it comforting that commerce continues despite the state of emergency.

Angel drives slowly northward, weaving around debris and cars ditched when drivers lost their sight. He's headed for China Basin, where FEMA has set up its command trailers just beyond the ballpark. A Navy hospital ship up from San Diego dwarfs the adjacent right-field wall. It's not far to Maerskton. Sam would like nothing better than a shower, but he is mindful of Cayman's warning to avoid going home.

Further up, orange cones and construction lights are in bloom. Officials clad in matching vests wave the semi onward, alerted to the truck's precious cargo by the manifest transponder. For Irish Protestants, the color first symbolized a personal authority, William of Orange, before becoming their brand of divinity; for Americans, it's dominion in the abstract, the shade of both the carrot and the implied stick.

Most of the twenty thousand people already in line outside SlimNow Park can't see their DayGlo federal shepherds. But they're nonetheless compliant. They want new eyes. They're eerily quiet while they wait, dependent now on sound. Friends and relatives fortunate enough to be asymptomatic run interference, checking on the estimated wait time and serving as guides. Over the whispers, pushers make themselves heard, selling food and pharmaceuticals to the captive audience from pushcarts.

With a nod to Angel, Sam climbs down from the truck and stretches. He's standing on a loading dock of pristine asphalt. To the east, a concrete pier extends toward the rising sun. Coins of water at his feet catch the dawn. He watches for a moment as medical workers in moon suits swarm around and begin unloading the iced eyes. Then he wanders off to search for caffeine.

"Marilyn, where's the nearest place I can get some coffee?" he asks.

"Your location data is unavailable," Marilyn responds.

"Report error code," Sam demands.

"Error: Diagnostics restricted."

It's one thing to be told there's a wall up ahead; it's another to run smack into it. Not that he's ever loved the network. But it worked in obvious ways, at least. It was transparent. Now no more. And that's troubling.

"So that's how it's going to be, Marilyn? We're keeping secrets?"

"I don't understand your question, Sam."

Sam doesn't elaborate. He spots Luis up ahead, leaning on his umbrella, gazing eastward toward the sunrise.

"Morning, Luis," he says as he approaches. "You look like you're posing for a movie poster."

"Just admiring the view."

"You're immune?"

"Or lucky. Whatever. I can see fine."

Sam stands next to Luis and gazes eastward. The Oakland hills seem to burn beneath the dawn. "It looks better through new eyes," he says, without meaning it.

"You had the operation?"

"Not by choice. That's a crime, isn't it, when someone takes your eyes?"

Luis cocks his head. "Organ theft. There's a specific statue dealing with it. The Organ Theft Prevention Act."

"I thought that was a trade bill to protect tissue growers. Something to stop cheap organ imports."

"It also includes penalties for unlicensed harvesting or donation. That's how these things get passed. They include a ban on something that resonates with the public and no one bothers to read the rest of the bill. My favorite is the Kitten-Crushing Prohibition Act. It's really about forbidding the disclosure of outbreaks among livestock, to protect meat industry sales."

Sam isn't listening. "Harris Cayman stole my eyes," he says.

Luis steps back and looks directly at Sam. It's evident that he's skeptical, but at least he hasn't dismissed Sam's claim wholesale. Finally, he just shakes his head.

"The past two days have been chaos here. We're just getting things back under control. If you catch Mr. Cayman offing 'gents with a shotgun here in the city, I'll see what I can do. Until then, I've got things to deal with."

"I understand," Sam says coldly.

Luis shrugs. "I wish I could do more."

Sam looks at Luis and no longer sees a friend. Not that they were ever close. But they'd shared something, a common interest in the practical, diluted sort of truth and justice that works in the real world. "Just show me what the machine came up with."

For tax reasons, the Solve-O-Matic has its own office at the Lease-4-Less facility on Bryant Street, where the bulk of the city's municipal law enforcement contractors have set up shop. The utilitarian beige computer hunkers atop a battered desk with no chair, beside its flatscreen display. Though its internals are smaller than a pack of cards, it's about the size of a toaster. This is the result of market research that correlates apparent volume and perceived value—important data for inflating state contracts. There's a Tesla coil tethered to it, bubbling with electricity, possibly the work of a Mary Shelley fan—or simply a tech with a sense of the absurd.

The authorized Solve-O-Matic site specialist, a gnomish, bearded man named Percy, greets Luis and Sam. He makes it clear he didn't enjoy rising early for this seven a.m. meeting. He produces a dongle from his pocket and plugs it into the machine before initiating voice authorization. Once logged in, he instructs the machine to display how it determined that George Gannet murdered Dr. Mako.

Two columns cascade down the screen:

Last Name:	Gannet
First Name:	George
Overflow Name:	None
Alias:	None
DOB:	November 11, 2007
Method of Identification:	Biometric, Genetic
Global Reference Number:	3AF562E0772B
Criminal Case Link:	SF/CA/USA: 30119887
Legal Representation:	Statutory, Expert System
Charge:	Murder, First degree
Claim:	Innocence
Alibi:	Pending
Synchronicity:	+04:01:23
Likelihood of Guilt:	92.031%

Likelihood of Conviction:	99.999%
Forensic Evidence:	Pending
Witness Testimony:	Pending
Video Surveillance:	None
Audio Surveillance:	None
Device Surveillance:	None
Past Offenses:	Battery; Loitering
Past Associations:	Pending
Family Connections:	None
Monoamine Oxidase A:	Low
D4 Dopamine Receptor:	Exon III Polymorphism
Religious Affiliation:	Pending
Political Affiliation:	Pending
Union Affiliation:	Homeless Union
Income:	Poor
Police-Related Philanthropy:	None
Race:	Caucasian
Ethnicity:	Western European
Lifestyle:	Indigent
Appearance:	Unappealing
Viewing Habits:	Pornography
Reading Habits:	Pending
Listening Habits:	Classical
Purchasing Habits:	Insufficient
Outstanding Parking Tickets:	None

Other:	Classified
Proj. Legal Cost:	($523,000)
Proj. Length of Sentence:	18 years
Proj. Years of Life Remaining:	12 years
Proj. Incarceration Cost:	($4,800,000)
Proj. Revenue While Imprisoned:	$8,280,000

Sam scans the screen and snorts. "That's it?"

Luis looks to Percy. Percy is not laughing.

Exasperated, Sam continues, "The Synchronicity score is four hours! The box can't place him at the scene until four hours after the crime, and it still rates Gannet as guilty?"

"There's other data to consider," Percy points out. "The genetic factors alone make me highly suspicious."

"For chrissake, the forensic evidence is pending!"

"That just means not all the relevant data has been entered," Percy counters. "When the likely statistical variation is less than the difference between the working tally and the guilt threshold, the Solve-O-Matic makes a determination."

Sam jabs a finger at the screen. "What's 'Other'?"

"That's classified."

"I can see that. How much weight does 'Other' get in the final tally?"

Percy folds his arms. "That's classified too."

Luis excuses himself to answer an incoming call and steps out into the hallway.

Sam paces. He looks at Luis outside, at Percy, and then

at the Solve-O-Matic. "Where's Gannet being held?" he asks, turning so that Luis won't hear.

Two hours later, after protracted negotiations with the Homeless Union's legal team, Sam receives permission to interview George Gannet. Then it's a short hop to Colma by air taxi in the company of Wu Hen, a newly minted attorney representing the Union. Despite his youth, there's an air of confidence about him, and Sam gets the impression that this job is a stepping-stone along the path toward greater ambitions.

They arrive at De-Tiny Containers, a self-storage facility for law enforcement agencies and contractors that's used for detainee containment. The cells are small enough to prevent prisoners—"clients"—from straightening out when they lie down. This is contrary to federal guidelines for penal service providers, but as De-Tiny CEO Ghent von Otter likes to say, "Cramped quarters keep clients thinking outside the box."

Tucked behind a hill, just down the road from a landfill, De-Tiny's boxes are stacked in groups three high and three long on a muddy flat that used to be a drive-in. Temporary hookups providing water and power bristle from the ground.

Sam takes an immediate dislike to the place because it's built with shipping containers; it's just like home, but subdivided further. He follows Wu, zigzagging to avoid the worst of the mud, and comes finally to an earth-toned container away from the others. The industrial lift that presumably removed it from the stacks sits off to the side. There's a bot waiting by the door of Gannet's cell. It's a Russian-made model from Stalin

Corporation that resembles a lawnmower fitted with treads, camera, and machine gun.

"State your business," the bot says without inflection.

"We're here to interview George Gannet," Wu answers. "Authorize."

There's a moment's pause. "Recognized," it responds. There's a click as the cell door unlocks. "Granted: Fifty-foot freedom of movement. Do not exceed this limit."

Wu opens the door and bends to address the huddled occupant of the container. "Mr. Gannet, I'm Wu Hen, your union counsel. Mr. Crane here wishes to ask you some questions. Based on what's he's told me, I believe it would be in your best interest to cooperate."

Gannet emerges slowly, unfolding himself like a hermit crab. He smells of the sewer. His filthy face is bruised. He's a big man with the eyes of a beaten child. He looks familiar.

"Hello," Sam says.

Gannet nods, squinting, eyes turned toward the sky as if it is about to fall.

Looking at his scab-striped hands, Sam immediately thinks defensive wounds. Then he remembers, and for a moment forgets to breathe. "I know you," he says, echoing the words Gannet shouted. "That's what you said to the FBI agents you attacked. How did you know them?"

Gannet points to his head, index finger and thumb mimicking gun barrel and hammer. "I see things," he mutters.

"What things?"

"Things that aren't there."

Marilyn chimes in, "Dr. Donut is just around the corner.

The coffee is hot and the donuts are to die for. Can I tempt you to try one?"

The armed lawnmower whirs and swivels to face Gannet. "Warning," it drones. "You have overstepped your bounds. Return to the safe area or you will die. You have zero seconds to comply."

A burst of machine-gun fire tears Gannet to shreds. His body collapses backward, leaving a blood-splatter shadow on the container behind him.

The bot whirs, pivots on its treads, and goes still.

Raking his hair with a shaking hand, Wu staggers back.

"What the…" Sam starts to say, words trailing off, heart hammering.

Outside the container that serves as an office when De-Tiny management conducts site visits, a clutch of officials huddle in a semicircle. They're staring intently at a monitor on a card table as it replays Gannet's death. On screen, Gannet's blood looks bright red; on the container, it's already sun-baked brown.

There's an officious-looking rep from MEs4U, a company that supplies both medical examiners for crime scenes and antibacterial consultants for the burgeoning population of germ-phobics. Nial stands beside Sam, squinting at the display. Luis is there too. Toward the back of the pack, two officers from his crew crane their necks to get a better view. A De-Tiny VP cups her earpiece with her hand, conversing with someone at the corporate headquarters about licensing video of the incident and the effect on liability costs. There are a handful of others too—reporters looking for details that will confirm the biases of their publications and public-relations reps trying to tailor the truth to please their clients. Apart from Luis, everyone looks somewhat disheveled and sleep-deprived from dealing with the outbreak.

The only actual government employee present is an elderly man from the Occupational Safety and Health Administration. Had a human murdered Gannet, federal lawyers would be here in abundance. But the path of least resistance at the moment seems to lead to the conclusion that Gannet died in an industrial accident.

The real work here will be undoing the brand damage to Stalin Corporation. One of the robotics company's technicians takes a step in that direction by announcing that the machine is functioning properly. "The problem appears to be with the Absolute Positioning System. Somehow, the geolocation data got corrupted and the unit thought the prisoner was outside the perimeter."

"If the unit actually thought," Sam says, "it might have made some effort to investigate the fact that it had apparently teleported to a new location."

"But it doesn't think," the technician retorts. "It did as it was told."

"It was only following orders."

The technician folds his arms. "It obeys its code," he says.

"You could also say it executes its code," Sam counters. "But clear that with PR before you try it."

The woman from De-Tiny moves through the group. She walks slowly, constrained by surgically tightened skin. Her suit hugs her like a sausage casing. She takes Sam aside, her hand on his shoulder. He notes resentfully that the others seem appreciative.

"I'm Karen Colt," she says. "Vice President of Public Relations."

In no mood to help her out, Sam nods. "Okay."

"And you're Sam Crane, I believe?"

"That's my impression, too."

"I understand you witnessed the incident?"

Again, Sam nods.

Karen shows scripted concern. "And after what happened to your wife," she laments. "This must be difficult. Have you considered seeing someone to talk about the trauma?"

Her eyes recall oncoming headlights. The car accident that killed his wife plays in Sam's memory. It's an ad for caution, if such a thing could be boxed and branded like perfume. Karen must have seen his psych records somehow. She's laying the groundwork for a litigation strategy based on mental instability: Shut up or face the pills.

Sam seizes her arm. He wants to break it. He can't help himself. But he realizes too late that his show of force only weakens his position.

"You're hurting me!" Karen exclaims for all to hear.

Sam lets go, ashamed. Assaulting women isn't his style, he tells himself.

"I realize this has been difficult," she says with a grimace. "It would be worth your while to seek counseling."

On cue, the sympathetic face of Dr. Amelia Katz appears, transparent, over Karen's shoulder. Sam knows the doctor's name because it's written in a white sans-serif font beneath her image, along with her specialty, chemical psychiatry. Then the graphics begin to fade.

Sam rubs his eyes as if he could wipe the characters away. He casts an accusatory glance at Nial, but it goes unnoticed. He finds it odd Nial is here at all; it was Luis who arrested Gannet, after all. But it's hard to believe Nial would rat him out in retaliation for being decked so long ago. Between Cayman and the Feds, anyone could have tipped Karen off to the presence of the word "volatile" in an old mental-health evaluation. Whoever is responsible, Sam sees he's been played.

"Maybe you're right," he says finally, pouring contempt into a smile. "I'm open to suggestions—as long as it's someone more competent than your plastic surgeon."

Sitting on the steps outside the San Francisco Public Library, Sam composes his advertisement for the replica of Dr. Mako's galvanic spectacles. He's using a disposable tablet, so he can't be immediately identified from his hardware license, and a temporary identity purchased from a street vendor. He rereads the descriptive text, then publishes the post. It's done.

Civic Center Plaza looks subdued. The 'gents encamped around the various government buildings move slowly, if at all. There are few pedestrians and fewer cars, apart from the armored one parked in front of City Hall. Umbrella vendors, normally scarce on sunny days, are out in force, capitalizing on the demand for makeshift canes for the blind.

Sam smiles for the street cameras; he should be easily recognized. He wants to be identified, just not immediately. If

Caddis—or anyone else—has spiders crawling the network, they'll be made aware of his post. But it will take time to pinpoint his location and confirm that it's him—processing video feeds for a facial-image match is slow—and by then he'll have moved on.

White letters scroll across Sam's field of vision. They read, "Well done, Mr. Crane."

Sam shakes his head as if a fly just landed on his face. He glares at the heavens, cursing under his breath. The letters turn orange, adapting to stand out against the sky. "Get out of my head!" he barks.

Passersby take no notice. It's as much disinterest as blindness. Erratic behavior is so often a scripted promotional event. Brawls to resolve the ongoing tastes-great/less-filling debate break out somewhere in the city at least once a day, under the watchful eye of a marketing rep.

More letters scroll across his field of vision. "Move along now. Your post has already been crawled. They will find you if you remain outside."

Casting his tablet into the trash, Sam heads toward BART. Surveillance feeds in the subway tunnels are only accessible to registered law enforcement organizations and carefully vetted sponsors, so Caddis shouldn't be able to track him there. As he rides the escalator down underground, something about the words he read in the sky bothers him. Then it hits him: Cayman, or whoever was keying in the text he saw, knew he was outside—they can see through his eyes.

Unbalanced by rage and revulsion, Sam reaches for the

handrail. He's shaking like a junkie. His eyes offend him, but plucking them out isn't an option.

Sam's self-pity is interrupted by the sound of air cars overhead. From the bottom of the escalator, all he can see is the ring of trash rippling outward in the draft of the descending rotors. There's a bit too much commotion up above.

Sam heads down the corridor toward the fare gate. There are fewer people around than usual, though that's hardly a surprise. Dance pop plays when he passes. Video billboards along the wall mimic mirrors. In their simulated reflection, he's wearing a Monsta Thug jacket and pants, trendily torn and treated with buckshot and blood. Charles Manson's voice reads the flashing onscreen text: "On sale now for only $999 at all Murderer's Row and Murderer's Row for Kids locations."

At the gate, Sam places his hand on the biometric scanner, its plexiglass plate murky with the oil of skin. An alarm sounds; the gate remains closed. He glances toward the bulletproof attendant's booth. It's empty.

The slap of shoes on stone echoes from the corridor behind him.

Text scrolls across his field of vision: "Danger!"

Sam vaults the gate and starts to run. The escalator is going up at the moment, so he descends the stairs to the platforms. As the rate of his footfalls increases, the ads on the walls skew toward fitness products and deodorant.

There's no train when he reaches the platform, but a breeze heralds one coming.

Two men in suits arrive at the top of the stairs, both of Asian descent. One points and pursues, taking the steps two-by-two. The other steps out of view, heading elsewhere on the upper level.

The overhead display flashes, "EMBARCADERO 1 MIN 9 CAR TRAIN." That's not the usual end of the line; apparently trains still aren't allowed to leave the city. Light floods the tunnel, resolving into two incandescent eyes.

Sam backpedals and then bolts toward the far end of the platform. A commuter with a bike watches, vaguely curious.

Passing another set of stairs, Sam wheels about and starts to climb. The second man arrives at the top. He shouts something in Chinese.

Sam pivots and resumes his run. In the support column to his left, something catches his eye: a fire extinguisher. He smashes the glass and grabs it, triggering an alarm bell.

The train, slowing, rolls past.

Fifty feet away now, the first man slows too, pulling a gun from his jacket. The second, similarly armed, has reached the bottom of the stairs and isn't far behind.

Sam ducks behind the column nearest his end of the platform.

The train stops; its doors slide open. Passengers peer out as the alarm wails.

"Weapons down, now!" someone shouts.

The two men stop.

Behind them, toward the middle of the platform, stands a BART security officer in firing stance. Moving behind the nearest support column, his partner takes aim as well.

The second man turns slowly, hands in the air. The first,

very still, mutters something, and the lights die. For a moment, the darkness is complete. Then the emergency backups kick in.

Something clatters on the platform.

The two pursuers are nowhere to be seen.

A stun grenade detonates in a blinding flash-bang. Passengers scream and scatter. The fire suppression system kicks in, triggering the sprinklers. The fire alarm continues in the rain.

Sam's ears are ringing, but he can see just fine; the flash doesn't seem to have affected his sight. Shifting to the other side of the platform, he peers out from behind his column, fire extinguisher at the ready.

The second gunman is charging right at him. A torrent of chemicals explodes in his face.

The man recoils and slips on the wet tiles. His gun fires a fléchette in the air. He tries to rise.

Sam steps up and punts the man's head, sending him sprawling.

Two gunshots come in quick succession. The first gunman emerges from behind a column midway up the platform and takes aim.

Sam tries to dive for cover behind the column. There's a shot and a stab of pain. He collapses, convulsing, with a small dart in his back.

His quivering frailty subsides shortly. The gunman is kneeling beside him, checking his pockets.

"The glasses," he demands in Cantonese-inflected English. "Where are they?"

All Sam can manage is a groan. As he lies on his back, words appear before his eyes: "Help is coming."

His interrogator stands suddenly and barks something at his prone companion. There's no reply; Sam's kick has left him unconscious.

Shouts echo from above.

The first man looks about, cursing. He says something to his agent and waits, looking impatient. He starts to back away.

There's a muted pop, like a champagne bottle opened within a coat. The second gunman's chest begins to smoke. He convulses briefly. Then a blinding magnesium flame bursts from his torso and consumes him. The air around him explodes as the brilliant white flames break blood and water into hydrogen and oxygen, feeding the fire.

"Joi gin," the first man says, grimacing as he turns away. In the nearest column, there's a door marked "Emergency Exit." He runs for it.

A half dozen riot police spill from the stairway in the middle of the platform and fan out.

Sam struggles to stand, backing away from the burning man. The stench of charred cloth and flesh makes him gag. With water streaming down his face, he fumbles for the fire extinguisher and points it at the flames.

Suddenly, everything looks red.

"Warning," Marilyn says. "This unit is not safe for Class D fires. Activating it will void your medical coverage and may expose you to civil and criminal liability."

The red tint fades.

Guns speak from the emergency-exit stairwell. Shouts

follow. Through the window of the stairwell door, Sam sees another magnesium fire flare up.

Within ten minutes, power and order are restored. The fire smolders under sheets of salt. Cleaning bots traverse the platform, scrubbing and drying the floor tiles as they go. The two BART security officers, wobbly but no longer stunned, manage the milling passengers. After tenting the charred corpses, the riot team plants laser wards on tripods to form a crime-scene perimeter. An announcer apologizes for the delay and promises train service will resume shortly.

Leaning against the wall at the end of the platform, Sam waits. He keeps his eyes closed out of spite, hoping to bore whoever is watching with him, whether it's Cayman or one of his lackeys. He'd like to put the whole incident behind him—or at least change into dry clothes—but he knows he can't just leave the scene.

"Mr. Crane, follow me, please."

Sam looks up at the riot officer armed with a submachine gun standing over him. He stands and stretches. His back still throbs where the fléchette struck.

The two take the elevator up. The top floor of the BART station is deserted except for a bomb-sniffing bot. The crackle of radios echoes from below. They pass through the fare gate.

It occurs to Sam to ask where he's being led.

"Debriefing," the officer says. "In here."

The officer opens a door and motions for Sam to enter.

Sam stops. Agent Gibbon waits inside, stiff and expressionless. The office is empty but for a table and four chairs.

A patch of brown, perhaps a coffee stain, mars the floor. Two long fluorescent bulbs bisect the ceiling. An air vent in the wall exhales like an asthmatic through a beard of dust.

Sam enters and takes a seat at the table. The riot officer leans on the wall beside the door.

"Nasty bump you've got there," Sam says to Gibbon.

"Would you like one?" Gibbon asks.

"Are you asking or threatening?"

"There's a difference?"

Sam shrugs. Making sure to keep the officer in sight, he sits down. "Where's your partner?"

"Getting new eyes."

Gibbon turns red for a moment—not flushed, but adjust-your-set red. Everything else in the room looks as it should. The word "Lie" appears over his head.

"So you're immune?" he asks, trying not to react to the distractions being beamed into his head.

"I had mine done yesterday."

"Yeah, they look a bit bloodshot," Sam observes.

"Turn off your log."

"Not after what happened last time."

Gibbon sighs. "Command, authorize Agent Gibbon. Terminate civilian logging at my coordinates. Over."

"Logging suspended," Marilyn announces.

A slight smile appears on Gibbon's otherwise impassive face. "Let's talk about glasses," he says.

"What would you like to know?"

"Show them to me."

"I don't have them on me."

"Where are they?"

Sam pauses, just to torment Gibbon. "Why do you want to know?"

"They're federal property."

"Since when?"

"Since the Bureau took over the Mako investigation."

"The Solve-O-Matic is going to be disappointed," Sam says.

"Pardon?"

"Never mind."

Gibbon shifts about in his chair. "So tell me where the glasses are," he says.

"I told you I don't have them."

"You can't very well sell them if they're not in your possession."

"They're in the care of someone else. I don't know who."

Cocking his head to the side, Gibbon seems to be listening to something. "Your voice-stress pattern suggests you're telling the truth."

"You sound surprised."

"Disappointed. I was looking forward to beating it out of you."

Stifling a smirk, Sam leans back in his chair. "So why were Chinese agents hoping to do the same?"

"I'm not here to indulge your questions."

The words "Stand slowly and quietly" appear over Gibbon's head. Sam hesitates for a moment, then complies.

Gibbon continues to look at the chair Sam just vacated. "I'm going to ask you one more time, Mr. Crane."

"Move to the door," the text advises.

Sam does so, the noise of the air vent masking his steps. The riot officer is standing next to the door. Both he and Agent Gibbon are still staring at the empty chair.

"Where are the glasses?" Gibbon asks one more time.

"Knock on the door," the text says.

Sam knocks.

The officer and Gibbon exchange glances. Gibbon gestures at the door. The officer opens it. Seeing no one, he steps outside. Without waiting for further instruction, Sam follows. Sensing something, the officer turns. Sam stops and tries to remain still. The officer's eyes look right through him. With a shrug, the officer returns to the room.

"There's no one there," he says as he shuts the door.

Emerging from the BART station, Sam heads east on Market Street toward the X Hotel, where the replica glasses are. In the sun and his jacket, he's sweating, but he's too preoccupied to remove his coat.

The street is surprisingly busy, considering the circumstances. Though the outbreak has reduced the number of cars on the road, there are quite a few pedestrians, not to mention soldiers. And of course there's no shortage of 'gents. Many of the panhandlers haven't yet adapted to the realities of begging from the blind; they're still holding cardboard signs that spell out their plight. But a few have taken to spoken or sung solicitations.

The fountain on the corner of Seventh and Market is one of two free water sources in the city. It features a statue of

Jurgen Spatz, the billionaire industrialist behind Municipal Water's parent company, Weltherschaft AG. Beneath a sign indemnifying the city and Municipal Water from health-related lawsuits, reasonably clean water pours from the copper-green statue's hands into a pool for anybody to take—though that's easier said than done. A loose ring of 'gents controls access to the water, which they bottle in scavenged plastic and sell for $5. Not to be outdone, City Water also maintains a public well downtown, a bit further east.

At Fifth Street, where commercial rents rise, the city changes. The downtown shopping area looks immaculate. To the west, buildings come with soot, faded paint, and cracked facades. The sidewalks are stained with gum, spit, trash, and grime. To the east, everything is unnaturally clean, as if the buildings sprang straight from an architect's computer rendering. Instead of loitering 'gents, fashionable citizens in business suits lean against the walls. Instead of ragged cardboard-box panels with copy crafted to tug on emotions and wallets, these well-to-do salespeople hold professionally printed placards for familiar products. The scent of lavender and lemon fills the air. Whenever Sam's gaze falls upon a storefront, a faint glow appears about the shop, distinguishing it from its surroundings.

Sam realizes how much of Cayman's vision layer is a work in progress. Having more or less come to terms with his visceral revulsion for mediated reality, he wonders how much control he has over what he sees. That, after all, is Cayman's selling point: the ability to create the world as you wish to see it. The trouble is that Sam's new eyes didn't come with a manual or tech support.

Turning south at Third Street, Sam finally reaches the hotel. The décor is stylish, with lots of black leather, dark wood, flowers, and terrazzo. Tight black turtlenecks—and the physique to look attractive in them—appear to be mandatory for the staff. Apart from a blind woman being helped through the revolving door by a soldier, there are few signs of the outbreak. He asks if there are any messages for Ryan Wolfe.

The receptionist shakes her head.

"Not surprising, with everything that's been going on," Sam says. "How has it played out for you all?"

"Hectic," she answers.

"Was anyone on staff affected?"

"Oh yeah. Not me for some reason. I feel really lucky."

"Enjoy it while it lasts." Sam heads for the elevators.

Room 451 is small but well-appointed. A red gift box tied with a white ribbon sits atop a brown bed. Sunlight seeps through the shutters.

Taking a seat on the bed, Sam opens the box. A hard black case inside houses the spectacles. The replica looks just as he remembers the genuine article. He tries them on. The rose-colored lenses show him a pleasant world, though the glasses are just slightly too heavy to be comfortable. He returns them to their case.

Marilyn breaks her silence to pitch Sam on the virtues of the minibar. Sam finds it interesting that while Cayman's system overrides many of the network ad buys, his agent still accepts and delivers site-specific solicitations like the ones provided by the hotel. Opening the waist-high fridge, he grabs a sandwich in cellophane and a bottle of Vater—tap water transformed with a trademark and bottled by the Global Cola Company. Cayman is picking up the tab, after all. And somehow it makes him feel altruistic to buy what his agent is selling.

Sam watches the news while he eats. It seems there have been outbreaks in cities all over the globe. A CNN reporter details the impact of blindness on a number of prominent actors. The cameras track every tear in close-up. Occasional cutaways to scenes of international chaos appear as dramatic punctuation. The logo of the underwriter, pancake and munitions chain FlakJack, has been superimposed on billboards and walls in the scenes of urban rioting.

The sight of unrest brings Fiona to mind. Sam directs Marilyn to put his daughter on screen. Her picture appears. She looks untroubled, which is especially comforting given what's happening in the outside world. He watches her for several minutes before signing off.

Sam asks Marilyn whether Tony Roan is at home. She answers that is he is. He starts to ask her to call him, then changes his mind. Some stories are best told in person.

A quick shower does little to relax him. He's anxious for Caddis to make contact.

"Thank you for using Municipal Water," Marilyn says through the bathroom speaker as Sam towels off. "Our records show that you use an alternative water provider at home. We'd like to have you as a customer, and to help that happen, we're offering a special one-time discount of two hundred seventy-nine a month for the next three months. Just say, 'It's a deal,' and we'll switch you over from your current provider at no extra charge."

Sam declines and gets dressed. That's when the call comes in.

Sam directs Marilyn to put the feed on the wall screen, but the video portion is only a placeholder graphic.

"I wish to inquire about the glasses you advertised," says the distorted voice of Emil Caddis.

"You're being much more polite than the last time you asked," Sam replies.

A pause. "The last time?"

"When you pushed me out of an airplane, Emil."

Caddis chuckles. "Sam Crane," he says. "I should have known."

"You sound like you're having technical issues."

"It's necessary to conceal my location. Let us talk terms."

"The glasses for the girl," Sam answers. "You know the score. We use a Korean DMZ escrow vault. I'm working with the Seoul branch of International Hostage Brokers."

"Twenty-four hours?"

Sam thinks about it for a moment. "Assuming I can get out of the country, that's fine."

"Until tomorrow, then."

"Wait. I want an explanation. What's so important about the glasses?"

"They have great sentimental value."

"Call terminated," Marilyn announces.

Sam spends the next hour making travel arrangements. There are no commercial flights out of San Francisco International due to the quarantine. But charters are allowed, with government approval. Marilyn manages to book him a flight at six p.m.—a bit too easily as far as Sam is concerned.

With his plans set, Sam takes a moment to relax on the bed. His thoughts drift back to the murder of George Gannet and he realizes what's been bothering him about the incident. He's certain Gannet must have been arrested on Wednesday after attacking agents Gibbon and Indri outside the Pure Café. But Luis said Gannet was picked up on Friday. It doesn't make sense that the FBI would let Gannet go so Luis could pick him up two days later. "I know you," he'd said. "I see things." Was that a revelation or a complaint? Had he been killed because he saw Mako's killer? Or was that his explanation for hallucination? Who's to say how Indri and Gibbon appeared to him if he saw them through another's eyes?

"Marilyn," Sam says, "Contact Wu Hen. I'd like to speak with him."

There's a brief pause. "Contact denied. His agent says he is on vacation and won't return until null days."

"That's a long vacation." In Sam's experience, missing data like that is a sign of manual tampering. So much for the easy road to Gannet's medical records. He could go directly to the medical examiner, but that seems risky at the moment. He decides to appeal to a higher power.

"Marilyn, contact Harris Cayman."

Another pause. "Contact denied," Marilyn repeats. "Inadequate privileges."

"I'm here, Mr. Crane," Cayman says. His voice sounds thin, as if he was speaking on a twentieth-century telephone.

Sam sits up, eyes glancing about the room as if searching for a mosquito. For all the absurdity of Cayman's God complex, there's something to his delusions. His omnipresence is unsettling.

"How long have you been watching?"

"There's always someone. I joined when Emil called."

"I see."

"You're going to have to move soon," Cayman continues. "Our efforts to conceal your location have failed."

"George Gannet," Sam says. "He had your eyes, didn't he?"

"Who is George Gannet?"

"Look him up. From San Francisco."

"A moment." The background hiss from Cayman's mic drops out, then returns. "There was a 'gent by that name in our alpha test. Very perceptive of you."

"Was he a willing participant?" Sam asks with an edge on his voice.

"As much as anyone bound by poverty is free in his choices."

"For how long?"

"Several months."

"How does it work? Is there a central control room?"

"I am at one of several control rooms," Cayman explains in paternal tones. "But control is a misnomer. The system is designed so there can't be any single point of failure. Access is sold through competitive bidding."

"How closely do you monitor your engineers?"

"You're suggesting we have a mole?"

"Well, if you weren't repainting Gannet's world, someone else was."

A pause. "I will have to look into it."

Sam stands and paces, rebelling against so much disembodied interaction. "I want to see," he demands. "I want to see what Gannet saw."

"Mr. Crane, I must insist that you focus on your assignment. Once Amy is safe, we can negotiate further."

"No." Sam is adamant. "I want 8:00 p.m. to 8:10 p.m, Monday, May 2."

"There isn't time for this."

"Make time. Or is that beyond your powers?"

"I can save you time, but I cannot give you more." There's an edge in Cayman's voice. "Government agents are approaching the hotel."

"Whose government?"

"Does it matter?"

Sam steps to the window and opens the shutters. Four men wearing suits, sunglasses, and sidearms are moving with purpose toward the hotel. They're walking in the right lane of the street, undeterred by the occasional car.

"It matters to me," Sam answers. "I live here. That becomes a lot harder if I'm wanted."

"They want the glasses, not you. You must leave now."

"Alright, alright," Sam says, grabbing his jacket. Struck by Cayman's apparent desperation, he steps into the hallway outside his room, deliberately leaving the replica glasses in their case on the bed.

"Take the stairway," Cayman says.

At the door to the stairwell, Sam suddenly stops. "The glasses. I forgot them."

"Back! Quickly!"

"Can you send me another copy?"

"No, no, no! Run, get them! They can't know the glasses are fake."

Sam turns and runs back toward the room.

"They're in the lobby," Cayman says.

A woman's voice can be heard addressing Cayman: "Elevator three will arrive first."

The door unlocks with the application of Sam's thumb.

"Sam," Cayman says, "I'm going to hand you off to our senior overseer. Jenny is more experienced with remote operations than I am."

"On station," Jenny says in a voice both confident and compelling. "I'm accessing the local surveillance nodes. You'll see them live in a sec."

Sam runs in and grabs the glasses from the bed. Cayman's insistence that he retrieve them makes him certain they contain a tracking device, or perhaps an explosive. He hurries back into the hallway and toward the elevators.

A semitransparent video window into another portion of the hotel appears in the upper right quadrant of Sam's field of vision. He's looking through the lens of a surveillance camera in the lobby. He watches two agents step into an elevator.

"Marc," Jenny says, "I need to know which ones have the sight."

"Already on it," a man's voice says in reply.

Sam turns toward the door to the stairs at the end of the hall. The view from the surveillance camera changes to reveal the bottom of the stairwell. Two more agents are climbing the stairs.

"Back to the elevators," Jenny says. "Quickly, press the up button. There's one approaching the fourth floor."

The feed in Sam's eyes cuts back to the two agents in an elevator.

Almost as soon as Sam presses the button, the elevator to his left opens. He steps in immediately, joining a uniformed waiter and a rolling cart moguled with the domes of plate covers. As the doors slide closed, he can hear the adjacent elevator opening. In his private cutaway window, he watches as the two agents arrive in the hallway he just left. Then the window fades.

The waiter produces a small bottle of Famished culinary perfume from his pocket, lifts the plate covers, and sprays the food concealed beneath a crispy fried coating.

Sam tries not to inhale, but fails. By the time the elevator reaches the seventh floor and the waiter exits, it takes all of Sam's will not to waylay the cart for himself.

"Press two," Jenny says. "Get off there and take the stairs to the lobby."

Sam complies. The elevator descends. "Can't you just make me invisible to them like before?" he asks.

"Not if they have a good overseer," Jenny answers. "I'd overlay and they'd counter by dropping the opacity to zero or switching to direct input. And not everyone has the sight yet."

The elevator stops and the doors open.

Sam steps out onto the second floor and runs down the hallway toward the door to the stairs. Video from the surveillance camera in the stairwell appears to the right of the door.

"The stairwell is clear," Jenny says.

The surveillance overlay piped to Sam's split-screen eyes still says the same thing. But the stairwell is not empty. Opening the door, Sam finds an agent standing on the landing above him.

The agent turns to look at Sam.

"Run, Sam!" says Jenny. "Get outside."

"Stop!" the agent demands.

Sam hurtles down the steps.

The agent follows, footfalls jackhammering the concrete.

"Seal the area," the agent shouts. "He's in the stairwell."

On the ground floor, Sam stops. In front of him stands a concrete wall. There's no way out.

"Where's the door?" Sam asks, frantic.

Looking back, the agent has vanished, his image deleted from Sam's view. Sam can still hear the slap of his shoes.

"I need an answer, Marc," Jenny says, her voice muffled, as if to conceal her desperation from her charge.

Confused, Sam faces the sound, raising his fists to fight.

"He doesn't have the sight, Jenny," someone says.

Jenny curses.

Then comes the impact, driving Sam back against the wall. Staggered, he lashes out, managing only a glancing blow. He swings again at the air.

"Stand by, Sam," Jenny says. "We're working on it."

The lights go out. Then they appear to come back on, sort of; Sam sees the darkened stairwell through a high-contrast filter. The agent shows up like a heat mirage. The masking layer that was hiding his form no longer blends with the background.

The agent looks disoriented as his eyes adjust to the darkness.

The door in the wall is now visible, and Sam takes it.

The lights are out in the lobby too, but with the contrast in his eyes boosted, the diffuse sunlight from the windows burns blindingly white.

Sam sprints, squinting, into the sun. The agent is close behind.

There's a hint of a doorman and a door ahead, silhouettes against the oversaturated daylight. Sam pushes through, stumbling over guests and luggage. Angry shouts follow. Then he's outside.

The agent collides with someone, but quickly gets back on his feet.

"Okay, Sam," Jenny says, "I'm imposing a static alignment map of the exterior. It will make the agent show up better."

The color contrast of Sam's world returns to normal. Then the buildings and other fixed objects darken and the moving elements—people, cars, trash, flags—suddenly stand out. Looking over his shoulder, Sam sees that the agent is visible too.

"Triple-O online," another voice says off-mic. "RUSSAT 3 good to go."

Jenny responds, "Take him out."

"The agent doesn't have the sight, Jenny. We can't get precise coordinates."

Another muted voice speaks, Cayman this time. "Make him sovereign," he orders.

"That's weird," says Jenny. "He was flagged but then got deactivated."

"That's the professor's file. Re-set the permissions."

Sam sprints west toward the convention center across the street. People are lined up there, presumably getting new eyes or supplies of some sort. Members of the National Guard can be seen nearby, but they don't seem to be aware of what the FBI is up to.

Marilyn recites, "Sam Crane, you have been granted Sovereign Operator privileges—"

"—Sam, you need to target—" Jenny interrupts, trying to talk over Marilyn.

"—Active weapon is—"

"—Stop, turn, and point at him—"

"—Kurograd Tetanizing Laser—"

Sam is running fast enough to trigger ads for athletic shoes on the variable display of a bus shelter he passes. The sidewalk is wide and there's no one near. Flags flying in a row above snap in the breeze. "You want me to stop?" he asks, confused.

"Stop, turn, and point at the agent," Jenny repeats. "Make sure he stays lined up with the tip of your finger."

Sam comes to a halt and wheels to face his pursuer. He extends his arm at the agent and points. A targeting reticle forms at the edge of his field of vision. After a moment's delay, it constricts around the obscured image of the agent's head.

"Keep focusing on him and say, 'Fire,'" says Jenny.

Sam obeys. The agent collapses in spasms and goes still.

Across the street, someone in a suit and tie devotes a curious glance to the fallen man before continuing on.

"Neat trick," Sam mutters.

"Keep heading west, Sam," Jenny says. "The rest are on their way."

Once more, Sam starts running. When he's about three-quarters of the way down the block, the remaining agents emerge from the hotel.

"There's an air taxi approaching the intersection ahead," Jenny says. "Take it."

Breathing heavily, Sam reaches the end of the block. To his right, an air taxi approaches along what would ordinarily be a busy street. He hails the cab and gets in.

"Where am I going?" Sam says to Jenny.

"You asking me?" the driver replies with a thick Ukrainian accent, turning to address Sam. His cratered face is further furrowed by a smirk. A gold cross rests on a patch of graying chest hair in the V-shaped frame formed by his inadequately buttoned polyester shirt. The shirt is several sizes too small for the beer belly it struggles to contain. "This is not tourist drive."

"Just go," Sam answers, looking back down the street at the approaching agents. "I'm on a call."

The driver shrugs. The air car accelerates, heading south on Fourth Street.

"Jenny?"

No answer.

"Jenny? Are you there?"

"No reception," the driver says.

In the jumble of electronics grafted to the dashboard, Sam notices an active block box. "You know you can get in trouble if you're caught with a jammer," he says.

"You planning tell someone?"

"Nah, just saying."

"Don't say. And I don't say. No one getting caught, right?"

"Fine by me."

"You get privacy extra for free in this cab," he explains. "Is park."

Sam guesses that the driver means "perk." He doesn't correct the pronunciation. He leans back against the slick vinyl seat, staring at the lens mounted above the rearview mirror. "What about the video camera?" he asks.

"Is private log, for my protection."

"What do you file with the Department of Public Vigilance?"

"I have friend who sells dummy video," the driver confides. "Is much better. No reports to fill out when network doesn't like customer."

Sam grins, recognizing a kindred subversive.

"You first customer I have to today," the driver continues. "I drive by, no one sees me."

"Obviously you weren't affected."

"I take vitamins. You want that I keep going?"f

"No," Sam answers slowly. "I'd like to go to Hayes and Lyon."

CHAPTER EIGHT

CITY WATER SPONSORS the intersection of Hayes Street and Lyon Street. The road has been painted deep blue with gold letters that proclaim, "You're drinking City Water now." On a bench outside the corner laundromat, one of the water company's hulking customer retention agents, conspicuous in his blue and gold uniform, sits with a blue and gold bat in hand. Next door, a sign in the window of a Chinese-owned dry cleaner reads, "City Water flows here."

Several dozen people are waiting in line to have their eyes replaced, queued up at a bloodmobile that's been pressed into service as a mobile surgical unit. Two soldiers are supervising. Out in the street, a handful of kids are playing blind man's bluff without a blindfold.

Clouds course overhead, moving in from the sea. Sam

emerges from the cab. The breeze hints at a coming chill, but the air is warm still.

Halfway down the block, Tony Roan is presiding over a yard sale outside his restored Victorian, as he often does on weekends. Seated on his front steps, he's offering a few pieces of furniture for sale at impossible prices, just for the appearance of legitimacy, but his hacked dolls are the main attraction. He's demonstrating one for the neighborhood kids, a vintage twentieth-century G.I. Joe retrofitted to walk and talk like gun-fu superstar Miles Oreo.

"You can buff my Cadillac," the action figure snarls— a line that went through rigorous focus-group testing and, backed by a substantial marketing budget, became the most repeated phrase in the nation for about a week last year.

"Inselting," using an insult to sell a product, is all the rage among commercial copywriters and Hollywood script-writers—a good inselt can earn in all manner of free products and other perks that never show up on tax returns—and has spawned a number of books and seminars on technique in recent years. Inselts entered the vernacular through the work of Harris Cayman. Rather than paying people to make positive comments about clients and their products in the course of casual conversation, he favored a more subtle approach. Working with a few trusted locals, he encouraged them to replace the mention of general product categories such as "car" in their artful, elaborate slurs with specific brands such as "Chryslerbishi." Rappers, smack-talkers, and street poets were brought on board. It didn't take much to convince them to abandon antiauthoritarian sentiments like "Fight the power!"

in favor of consumption-friendly banter along the lines of "Gonna mess ya with my Tesla." When it was done, insults amplified by emotional associations with products became the shortcut to street cred.

"You want Kleenex with that Nuckle Sandwich?" the toy taunts.

Grins grace the faces of three teens watching from the sidewalk. Tony puts G.I. Joe on the ground and the little solider struts a short distance, delivers a spinning roundhouse kick, then folds its arms.

Tony looks up as Sam approaches. He's dressed for comfort rather than style. His eyes are completely bloodshot, as if he just had the operation. "Hello, Sam," he says, offering a restrained smile.

"Looks like a slow day," Sam says. "Usually there's quite a crowd here."

"Wonder why?" Tony volleys.

"New eyes?" Sam asks.

"Yeah. It's kinda creeping me out."

"Just wait until you find out about the undocumented features." Responding to Tony's quizzical expression, Sam continues, "I'll explain later. Can we talk in your safe room? I suspect I don't have much time."

Tony sends the neighborhood kids on their way, grabs the modified toys, and heads into his garage. Sam follows.

The safe room occupies the back end of the house. It's a windowless office built with radio-proof wallboard. Tony does his unlicensed tinkering there, surrounded by a workbench, some shelves, two stools, a mini-fridge, and a few cardboard boxes. The overhead light is unnecessarily bright for their new adjustable eyes.

Tony grabs two bottles of beer from the fridge and hands one to Sam. "It's been pretty weird the past few days," he observes. "I got the call to get my eyes fixed Friday morning. Most of the law enforcement people were done Thursday. It was way too efficient. It's like they were ready for this."

"You better sit down," Sam says, sitting down himself on one of the stools. "I've got some things to tell you."

Tony takes a seat and waits. In the distance, rotors churn the air.

As Sam ponders how to begin, something catches his eye. It's a hard black eyeglass case, sitting on Tony's workbench. Panicked, he reaches for his jacket. But the case is still in his pocket.

"What's wrong?" Tony asks.

Sam shakes his head. "For a second there, I thought those were my glasses."

"They are your glasses."

"What?"

"Yeah. I meant to mention them when we were down by the Ferry Building, but…"

Sam stands and grabs the case from the table. He opens it. The spectacles inside are identical to the decoy pair in his vest pocket.

"How did you get these?" Sam stammers.

"Jacob brought that little blue dachshund by last Monday—"

"Duke."

"—and wanted me to check his voice box," Tony explains. "Said his voice sounded distorted. Anyway, he mentioned that you'd given him these and he planned to auction them. But he wanted to me to run some scans first."

"And?"

"They're complicated. But I have a pretty good idea what they do." Tony leans forward. "Spread-spectrum cancellation."

"Spread-spectrum wave cancellation," Sam repeats, mulling the words. "For jamming network broadcasts?"

"That's probably the effect. But it's not jamming, technically. Jamming interferes with a signal in a larger area. Those glasses put out radio waves that cancel the network signal at a very specific location."

Sam's eyes widen. "Mako made himself the antidote."

"That's not all," Tony says. "They have a micro-emitter that could communicate with network nodes. I don't know what it does yet because I've been afraid to use them outside of this room."

Gingerly, Sam dons the glasses. All about him, a luminous representation of the network appears. It's as if he's stepped into an architectural model of the virtual world. His viewpoint changes as he moves his hands, zooming from an image of a house with local file storage to a map of network node traffic patterns rendered over the floor to a view of Earth and its legion of satellites.

Words appear in the air. "Root access enabled. Waiting for network authentication."

"Wow," Sam says slowly. "The key to the kingdom."

"What?" says Tony, now multihued beneath layers of semitransparent graphics.

Sam struggles to respond. "That's what Harris Cayman meant. The glasses function as an authentication key. I'm seeing interface elements all around me."

"Really? I didn't see anything when I tried them on."

"Maybe because…" Sam stops as the answer dawns on him. "It's because don't have the right eyes." Shuddering, he reaches up and pulls the glasses off. Nothing changes. He instinctively waves his hands in front of his face, and the interface fades.

"Why would yours?"

"Because they're not mine. They were…how shall I put it…installed without my consent, courtesy of Harris Cayman."

"Get out of here," Tony exclaims, slack-jawed.

Sam spreads his arms, as if to show he has nothing to hide. "I'm quite serious. It didn't occur to me that I'd been given specific eyes for safekeeping. Unless I'm totally delusional, I'm looking through Xian Mako's eyes."

"Are they yours now, or are you just a mobile eye bank?"

Grimacing, Sam shakes his head. "Good question," he answers. He starts to put the glasses back on, but then it occurs to him they're no longer necessary—the door they unlocked is open. With another gesture, he recalls the interface.

Dr. Mako's virtual workspace appears once more. The gesture command system proves to be surprisingly intuitive. After a few moments, Sam is flailing his arms like a traffic cop to navigate the data sources. To his amazement, the interface seems to anticipate his directions; he realizes the system is wired to take its input from his motor-control system.

Tony chuckles. "What are you doing?"

"Navigating. There's a satellite-weapons control dashboard here, but it's offline."

"I would hope so," Tony answers. "We're in a shielded room."

"Give me a second here," Sam says, scanning the digital files Dr. Mako stored in his eyes.

There are a surprising number of files related to business correspondence with Sinotech, some in English and some in Chinese. Though Sam is only skimming them, it looks like Mako was negotiating the sale of Synthelegy trade secrets.

An air car approaches. The drone of its rotors does not fade. It's not passing by; it's landing.

Sam looks toward the sound and then at Tony. "Company's coming." A wave of his hand banishes Mako's file interface.

Outside, a hailstorm of debris scattered in the downdraft of the descending air car clatters against the garage door.

Tony stares toward the street, his face furrowed with concern. "What have you gotten mixed up in, Sam?"

Stepping out of the safe room into the garage, Sam shouts over the roar, "Tell me you have a back door."

"Upstairs." Tony leads the way.

Back in radio contact with the network, Sam tells Marilyn to find Jenny.

Marilyn responds, "There's no one by that name in your vicinity or your contacts file. If you'd like to supply additional information, I will attempt to initiate contact."

Cursing, Sam emerges from the basement behind Tony. To his right are the kitchen and the back door. To his left, outside the front door, boots slam against wooden steps. He knows he should run, but he doesn't.

"Hold on, Tony," he says. "They'll probably catch me and they're certainly going to hassle you. I don't want you to get dragged into this."

"Too late for that," Tony protests. "I'll…try to hold them off."

Sam grabs Tony by the shoulders. "With what? Wake up, Tony. I'm trying to do you a favor. I owe you more than one."

A voice from outside shouts, "Sam Crane, come out or we come in."

Sam glances toward the street then back at Tony. "The whole reason I came here was to ask you to look after Fiona if something happens to me," he says. "She's not much trouble."

In the short silence between the two men, much is said. Finally, Tony answers with a nod. "No trouble at all, Sam."

"I appreciate it." Drawing a deep breath, Sam musters something of a smile. He then recalls Mako's files with a thought. They appear about him like leaves lifted by the wind. He tries to focus on the one with a satellite graphic, but it doesn't respond to his will. He's having trouble concentrating. Reaching out to open it proves more effective.

Tony is staring at him, fascinated.

"I'm hooked to this orbital artillery system," Sam explains. "I'm trying to figure the damn thing out. I have this remote operator who has been helping me out but she seems to be offline."

"Orbital artillery? You're joking?"

"I'm not."

A settings menu unfurls in the air, draping the hallway wall. It reads:

Fire Control Mode: Sovereign

Active Weapon: Kurograd Tetanizing Laser

Fire Source: RUSSAT3

Targeting: Pinpoint

ECCM: Disabled

Reactive Suppression Fire: Disabled

Predictive Tracking: Enabled

Preemptive Defense: Disabled

Target Verification: Disabled

Collateral Damage Minimization: Disabled

Observe Treaty Limitations: Disabled

From outside, the voice shouts, "Sam Crane, you have sixty seconds."

"Marilyn, can you enable Collateral Damage Minimization?" Sam asks.

"Setting saved," Marilyn says. "Is your life insurance up to date, Sam? For a limited time, TGC is offering a low monthly premium of $129,000,000.99. Act now before it's too late!"

"No, Marilyn, I don't want life insurance from The Gambling Company," Sam responds aloud.

"I think she's is trying to tell you something," Tony observes.

Sam shrugs. "Any time there are more than three law

enforcement officials in one place, the local risk index goes up."

"That much?"

"Don't worry," Sam deadpans. "I won't blow up your house."

"Please don't even joke about that."

"It'll be safer for everyone if I'm rid of these."

Sam removes the black glasses case—the one with the decoys—from his jacket and holds it over his head as he steps outside. He waits on the landing outside Tony's front door.

Scores of agents fill the street below, bristling with weapons. There's something about their movements that suggests computer coordination. Like the algorithmically generated crowds in movie epics, there's an inorganic quality that undermines the illusion. Sam surmises most of the agents are decoy projections. Amid the troops, several government air cars block the street.

Two pedestrians stroll past, oblivious, as if nothing of note was happening.

"On your knees," commands one of the agents. "Drop your weapon."

Sam recognizes him immediately: Dr. Stephen Ursa. "I believe this is what you're looking for," he says, holding up the black glasses case. "I am going to walk down the stairs and place these glasses on the sidewalk. You're going to take them. And then you're going to go."

"That's not the way we do business," says Stephen.

"I suggest you consider a policy change, then," Sam says, descending the steps. "If you're here for the glasses, they're yours. If you're here to arrest me because you want a trophy, it's not going to go as well."

"We don't bargain, Mr. Crane."

As if on cue, arms tense, clothing rustles, and weapons click. Gun barrels stare back at Sam. Unlike eyes, they see death without reflection.

"What's it going to be?" Stephen demands.

Sam longs to fight. The thought of being able to call down the wrath of the heavens is almost too much to forego. With a gesture from him, it would all end in fire. Cayman's words haunt him: "You call down God's damnation because you long for his power."

Sam knows he does. Yet, there's something more. Though he hears Cayman's words, he sees his daughter's face. More than God's power, he craves mercy.

At the bottom of the steps, Sam closes his eyes and kneels.

Hands slam Sam to the ground and pull the glasses case from his grasp. They bend his arms back and tie them with plastic restraints. Someone slips a Faraday bag over his head to isolate him from the network. It smells like sweat and metal. Forcing him up, the agents maneuver him toward and into a waiting air car.

Gyring skyward, bound and blind, Sam feels free.

After what seems an interminable wait, Dr. Ursa finally removes the bag from Sam's head. Up close, his surgically tightened skin suddenly makes sense; Sam now sees that he must have been burned at some point. The reconstruction appears to have been done well.

Sam is sitting in a small interrogation room with a stainless-steel table and two matching chairs. His hands are still bound behind his back. The scent of bleach is strong enough to sting. The room is bright and windowless. A single steel door offers the only way out. Stephen stands beside it.

"Why am I here?" Sam asks.

"Because we need to talk," Stephen answers.

"I'm getting tired of being questioned."

"This isn't an interrogation. It's a negotiation."

"Then would you mind untying my hands?"

"I don't have anything to cut the restraints at the moment." Stephen shifts his weight and folds his arms. "But your answers here will determine whether I am motivated to free you."

"I feel like a contestant on Who Wants Someone Else's Money?"

Stephen offers a polite smile, creating strange creases in his too-smooth face. "Do you recall asking me to put you on the payroll?"

"I say stupid things sometimes."

"Perhaps," Stephen concedes, "but that particular idea has merit now. We know a lot more than we did when last you and I spoke. You're our best shot at securing Amy Ibis."

Sam is puzzled. "I thought you were after Emil Caddis?"

"Oh, we are after Emil. We're always after Emil. He'll be eliminated as soon as we have Ms. Ibis. Get to her and we get to him."

"And how does Amy fit into this?"

"She's the key to Harris Cayman. You know that."

Sam glares. "What a low bunch of bastards you are."

Stephen nods. "Something you have experience with, I realize. If you want our help freeing Fiona, you'll do as we ask. Time is short and the stakes are high."

"Cayman is already keeping Fiona safe, so to speak."

"Who do you think has more pull, your government or a rogue advertising magnate?"

Sam waits a long time before answering. He decides to gamble on the building being radio-proof. "Show me that my daughter is safe and I'll cooperate."

Stephen beckons toward the door and Sam follows, hands still tied. They leave the cellblock and walk past blast doors and a guard bot into an expanse of shoulder-high cubicles. He asks a colleague for a pair of scissors and cuts the plastic ties binding Sam's hands.

Sam rubs his still-striated wrists. Surveying the maze of office dividers, he sees heads rise into view, move, then drop out of sight. It reminds him of the Whac-A-Mole game he played at carnivals as a child.

Handing the scissors back, Stephen asks the agent to show Sam the Zvista feed on his daughter.

"What room is your daughter in?" the agent asks.

"Room 305," Stephen interjects.

The FBI agent addresses his network agent. Fiona appears on the monitor, complete with a readout of all the patient diagnostic information that is supposed to be available only to parents, spouses, domestic partners, insurance companies, and pharmaceutical marketers. She seems so serene.

Sam watches for a moment, then nods. The image reveals

nothing; everything on the monitor could be faked. But he has to accept it. To do otherwise would lead to violence and probably his death. He turns away and says, "Okay."

The remote operations room in the downtown office of the FBI is impressive. Once an art-deco movie palace, it's now home to a sophisticated audiovisual nerve center dominated by three giant video screens that display live feeds from agents in the field. Over a dozen operators with earpieces, goggles, and feedback gloves provide assistance to those they're monitoring. Today, they're mostly watching the show. Several agents have bags of microwave popcorn.

Stephen explains that the operation on the central screen is being run directly by the CIA in Langley, Virginia. The intelligence agency is providing a feed to sister agencies as a courtesy. The image comes from one of the agency's drones in Venezuela.

Treetops scroll off the bottom of the screen. Afternoon sky fills the top. Jungle birds scatter. A clearing appears in the distance. There's a building there. It moves slowly closer. The jungle ambience sounds compressed.

A burst of white light fills the frame and the drone's exposure sensor tries to compensate. In the building's place stands a smoking ruin.

"OOO," one of the agents in the audience says with exaggerated awe, eliciting a few chuckles. Sam gets the joke. O.O.O. stands for Offensive Orbital Ordinance.

Faint voices echo. Panning its camera, the drone moves toward the sound. The screen fills with foliage. Then the colors change as the drone looks through different filters: thermal, infrared, and ultraviolet.

A man appears in silhouette. Then he falls down dead.

"OOO," gasps another agent, again prompting faint laughter.

The drone turns its lens to other areas around the destroyed structure, to make sure there are no survivors.

"That was the lab where we believe the virus was developed," Stephen whispers to Sam. "The President ordered a decisive response."

"The President Strikes Again," Sam quips.

"There are better ones in the series," Stephen says. "Ever seen The President and the Terrorist?"

Sam shakes his head. "I've never even heard of that one."

"You're living it," Stephen says. "Your part will be to go to Korea, just as you planned. You'll exchange the glasses for Amy. Once she is safe, we will eliminate Emil. After that, I expect Harris Cayman will be more cooperative."

Sam laughs.

"What's so funny?"

"You're asking me to do exactly what Cayman wants."

"No. Cayman wants Caddis' gun removed from his head. We want Caddis' gun so we can point it at Cayman."

"To what end?"

Stephen pauses to consider his words carefully. "The power he can grant diminishes the state," he says.

"Are you talking about the ability to control orbital weapons or the ability to control the look of the world?"

"Both. It should be obvious we can't have citizens running

around with the ability to call down air strikes," explains Stephen. "And it should be equally evident that freedom cannot be sustained without limits. The world is not yours to remake."

"Whose is it?"

Stephen just smiles and gestures toward the door. "You can go now. Your flight leaves in three hours. Don't make us come get you."

Sam starts toward the door, then stops. "Why are you letting me go?"

Stephen doesn't answer. "See you at the airport."

Just after four p.m., Sam emerges from the FBI building. He's dosed with Demendicil so Cayman can't detect his lies. He hopes the circuits in his new eyes don't monitor blood chemistry. He's all but certain the FBI is monitoring him.

Taking a seat on the stone steps, Sam waits for Cayman to call. Minutes pass in silence.

Traffic is still sparse. It feels like a holiday. Pigeons strut across the street against the light without consequences.

Sam wonders why he's free. It's true that the FBI, with all its surveillance equipment throughout the city, can locate him at will. But there must be something more to it.

"Marilyn," Sam says, "finger Tony Roan."

"He's busy."

"Doing what?" Sam is a bit annoyed.

"No explanation is available."

"Send him a voice message. Begin: Tony, I'm okay. I'm headed to Seoul tonight. I'll be in touch. End message."

"Message sent, Sam. Based on speech analysis, the network has determined that your call was unrelated to business. You will be billed at the social rate."

Sam rises and sets off toward Fisherman's Wharf. He's decided to try getting back to a world he understands, to being a spec. A few days ago, he had a relatively simple goal: finding out who killed Dr. Xian Mako. Somehow he's become a pawn in game that's beyond him.

The next few blocks pass without incident or interruption. It's a strange tranquility, like the calm before a storm. It's relaxing at first, the absence of ads, of people clamoring for attention. Then it becomes eerie. He begins to wonder whether he's missing something. He stops, closes his eyes, and touches the nearest building to compare its appearance to its texture. It feels the way it looks.

The wharf itself isn't entirely deserted. A handful of tourists, trapped in town by the quarantine, mill about amid shuttered stores. The mood is somber. A street performer sits on the edge of a public bench that has been designed with lumbar protrusions and seat ridges to minimize loitering by maximizing discomfort. Beside him lies a canvas bag stuffed with juggling props, but he seems unable to muster the energy to play for an audience.

Ikura Industries occupies a small storefront on Pier 33 amid the tourist traps and bombastic signage. Though hardly the largest wholesale fish outlet in the city, it has relationships with most of the local high-end seafood restaurants. A sign on the wall beside the door says, "Closed."

When Sam tries the door, it opens.

Inside, a middle-aged Japanese man sporting a goatee and pinched lips stands behind the counter. He's in the midst of an audio-only conversation. He lifts his hand to acknowledge Sam. A bowl of mints mummified in cellophane tempts the undiscerning. The strong scent of fish does little to make the candies more appetizing.

Eventually, the shopkeeper finishes his call and looks up. He listens politely to Sam's request to view his sales database, but immediately declines. "I'm sorry," he says. "That's proprietary information. You want to buy some fish? That's what I have to sell here."

"I'll buy a tale about who's buying fish."

The man shakes his head. "Sorry," he says again. "I can't help you."

"Uzai Sutaba?" Sam asks, recalling the owner's name from his network queries. "Is that right?"

"Yes."

"Well, Mr. Sutaba, you seem to be under the impression that you have an option," Sam explains, taking care to phrase his threat so that he can be understood but not sued. "You're operating under a state license. The state has a lot of regulations. One of them is that you open your database to criminal investigators upon request. I'm sure there are others, but it's awfully hard to remember them all."

Sutaba proves more receptive than Kenneth Wren. "I think we can work something out," he says, sliding a tablet across the counter to Sam and ordering his agent to grant access.

"Sen, show me a list of customers who purchased fugu between April 20 and May 2 of this year," Sam says.

The list is short; as Sam expected, most of the orders were from Aquamarine. But there's one individual name—someone Sam wouldn't have expected to be ordering on his own account.

Chef Shingen Saba's flat is just across the street from Golden Gate Park. It's a meticulously kept salmon-colored Edwardian. Normally, at this hour, Sam would have had to seek the chef out at Aquamarine. But the restaurant remains closed due to the outbreak.

Sam presses the doorbell and waits, hands clasped behind his back. His gaze wanders, entranced by the flashing stoplight suspended over the street.

From inside, someone shouts, "I told you I don't want to switch to City Water! Get out of here before I call the police."

"Mr. Saba? I'm here about Xian Mako."

The door opens. Saba is a stylishly dressed man, suspiciously slender for a chef. His eyes are post-op bloodshot. That alone would explain his evident disorientation.

"Mr. Saba, my name is Sam Crane," Sam explains. "I'm a spec. I'm investigating the death of Dr. Xian Mako on behalf of the police. I take it you know who he was?"

Saba nods, exhaling heavily. "Come in."

Removing his shoes, Sam follows the chef through a sparsely appointed foyer into the living room. Four imitation-Shaker chairs surround a glass coffee table. Though elegant, they prove uncomfortable. A reed mat covers most of the floor.

"Would you like something to drink?" Saba inquires.

"No, thanks." Sam notes Saba's agitated state. He waits a moment, sensing his host wants to talk.

"The preparation of that meal was flawless," Saba says suddenly. "I knew I should not have been doing it, but Miss Ibis wanted to surprise Xian and both have been good friends over the years."

"She asked you to prepare a dinner at her home?"

"Yes, and I was careful," Saba insists, then pauses. "I know they told me not to say anything."

Sam looks surprised. "Who told you?"

"Two men," Saba says. "They came to my kitchen and threatened me. I told them I wouldn't say anything."

"Do you know who they were?"

"They're all the same. They're criminals."

Sam nods. There's something compelling about Saba's defiance. He wonders what it is that makes him resist when others would be cowed. "So you prepared the fish properly. What happened to the liver and the skin?"

"I threw them away."

"Where they could be retrieved?"

Saba nods slowly.

Sam leans forward in his chair. "Do you believe Amy Ibis poisoned Dr. Mako?"

"Yes."

"Why would she do that?"

"They were lovers once. Hate comes easily after that."

Sam shakes his head to scold himself. How could he have not seen it? Was it because he felt something for her that he couldn't imagine her with Dr. Mako? Was it because he was Asian or she was rich? Or perhaps it was just that a lover's quarrel seems so prosaic amid the vastness of Cayman's conspiracy. "That night, did she seem angry with him?"

"There was some tension. I tried not to listen in. Xian was worried about a business deal in China."

"How much did he tell you about his work?"

"Very little. I don't think it was going well recently, though."

"What makes you say that?"

"He said he might be moving."

"I don't suppose you have your log from that evening?"

Saba shakes his head. "No, but I have the log from when the men came to intimidate me. I will send it to you."

"I'll see what I can do," Sam says. "In any event, I appreciate your candor. I don't expect any of this will get back to the licensing board."

Following a few more questions about Amy's and Mako's history, Sam thanks Saba and departs.

When Sam emerges, he sees Nial Fox in his trench coat leaning against his air car across the street. Behind him, the trees in the park bend in the breeze. Agents Gibbon and Indri stand close by, semi-transparent. They're looking at Nial but he takes no notice of them. Sam realizes they're hiding behind a masking layer. Mako's eyes see through it. Perhaps a hundred yards further west on the street, there's an FBI air car. Otherwise the street is empty.

Sam approaches, walking slowly across the street

without even checking for oncoming traffic. Nial shifts about. Something isn't right.

"What brings you out this way?" Sam asks.

"I heard the FBI picked you up earlier today," Nial answers.

"Word gets around." Sam notices the two concealed agents glance at one another. "Why do you care?"

"Did they ask about me?"

"Are you logging?"

Nial shakes his head. "This is off the record."

Sam waits before replying, watching the effect of the delay on Nial. He looks uneasy. Then again, his reflex implant would make it hard to stand still at the best of times. "You weren't mentioned," Sam says finally.

Nial suppresses a smile. "That's all I wanted to know."

"You could've just messaged me."

"Good policing is personal."

Sam doesn't buy it. He's thinking of Jacob's funeral, about the fact that Nial showed up at all. He's trying to remember the call he made to Nial from the freeway. What was it he said? "You're popping up on dispatch screens all over." It was as if Nial had been monitoring the dispatch feeds directly, with an attentiveness above and beyond the call of duty. And, on the night of Jacob's murder, Nial seemed certain no glasses had been found, but he showed no curiosity until Sam questioned him further. And what was the FBI looking for when it downloaded Nial's files?

"You know, I have a question for you," Sam says in monotone. "Why did you kill George Gannet?"

Nial barely reacts. "What're you're talking about?"

"That's what the Solve-O-Matic says," Sam continues, figuring that the Demendicil he took at the FBI office will hide his lie. "I asked Luis to give the box a crack at Gannet's case, just as a lark. And it came up with your name. It just seems like the sort of thing you might want to explain."

The silence is uncomfortable.

"You used Gannet to kill Jacob because Gannet had the sight," Sam says. "In his eyes, Jacob was someone else, someone he hated."

Nial sweeps his coat back and reaches for his gun.

It happens so fast Sam barely has time to react. He lunges forward, knocking Nial back onto the hood of his air car. The gun falls to the pavement.

Left arm holding Nial, Sam swings with his right.

Nial blocks Sams's blows with eerie speed. He rolls to the side, pulling Sam to the ground and knocking the air from his lungs.

Sam gasps as Nial stands.

Both men look for the gun. Sam sees two. The real gun, now camouflaged with graphics, looks ghostly; a projection of the gun lies nearby.

Aching, Sam rises. Gibbon and Indri draw their weapons.

Nial scrambles toward his weapon. He grabs for the pistol, but his hand passes through it. He grabs a second, then a third time. It's not there. He turns toward Sam.

Both men glare like gunfighters. But only one is armed.

Sam points at Nial and says, "Fire." A targeting reticle

forms around the detective. It closes about him and he collapses, wracked by spasms.

Sam can't help but smile.

Agents Gibbon and Indri lose their translucency. "Well done," Gibbon says with a flourish. "Did we startle you?"

Feigning surprise, Sam steps back. "Were you here the whole time?"

"We've been following you since you left," Gibbon answers. He pulls a restraint cord from his pocket and proceeds to bind Nial. "Command, terminate network access for Nial Fox."

"You were just using me for bait," Sam says.

"After your disappearing act in the BART station, I figure it's the least I could do."

"I guess you all are getting the hang of Oversight."

Neither agent recognizes the term.

"Cayman's overlay system," Sam adds. "That's why the gun appeared where it wasn't, right?"

"You mean the government's overlay system," Gibbon corrects. "We call it AVE. Augmented Vision Environment."

Sam looks surprised. "Only the military would propose such a neutered name," he says.

"No, only the Roman Empire."

"The what?"

"Sorry, ancient history." Gibbon says. "Let's go. I have orders to get you to the airport."

Nose pressed against hardened plastic, Sam admires the view from his window seat on Flight 761 to Seoul. Clouds emerge from concealment beneath the starboard wing, crawling as if on a conveyor belt. Below lies a gunmetal ocean. Standing in for the sound of waves, the air-conditioning system supplies a dull roar. Sam sees mile-wide letters floating atop the sea: "Ask your cabin attendant for a Sea Breeze made with genuine Oblivion Vodka."

The cabin reeks of chicken or pasta.

Sitting next to Sam are agents Indri and Gibbon. The former is snoring; the latter is enthralled by Sky Mall Magazine.

Sam passes a couple of hours watching The President Goes Hunting, in which the Commander-in-Chief's flight-simulator experience enables him to take to the skies in an F-22 and personally conduct air strikes against terrorists posing as atheist civil-rights attorneys.

Following the film, Sam declines an invitation from the two FBI agents to join a game of canasta. Instead, he logs into the network to review his notes and to see if he can get any further information on Nial Fox, now in federal custody. But his queries to Dr. Ursa and to Luis remain unanswered.

Upon landing at Incheon International Airport shortly after midnight on Sunday, Sam and the two agents endure several hours in a bio-containment area. When they're finally cleared, they find six men in similar suits waiting for them just beyond border control. Handshakes are exchanged; the group heads for a black SUV parked in a no-parking zone outside.

With heavy traffic around Seoul, the drive to the Joint Security Area Hilton at Panmunjom takes almost three hours;

civilian air cars are not permitted within fifty miles of the DMZ or the airport.

The JSA has been the site of rapid development since the sixtieth birthday celebration for North Korean leader Kim Jong-un in February 2043. Without addressing persistent rumors that Kim died from excessive consumption of cheese in 2014 and was replaced by a double, the Korean Central News Agency marked the occasion by announcing the publication of the Great Leader's latest statement of policy, "Implementing Juche Revolutionary Themes During My Sixth Decade." Though incomprehensible from a literary viewpoint, the attractively bound document did at least succeed as marketing: It carried an endorsement from Telomeritis, a leading maker of homeopathic anti-aging products. It was the first such official publication from the North Korean government to sport such sponsorship, an auspicious change in the eyes of the West. The new hundred-year plan called for "a revitalization of self-reliant socialism in the face of Western anti-humanism"—which North Korean government officials interpreted as a mandate to develop the country's tourist trade around the ransom industry.

Having never divined the fine line between kidnapping and tourism, North Korean tour operators have been seizing travelers around the globe with impunity for the past seven years. Following payment for meals (gluten-free, for a surcharge), accommodations, and deportation, DPRK guides escort their captives by train to the JSA, stopping along the way at staged villages for guided shopping breaks. Few can resist picking up memorabilia of their ordeal. At the conclusion of the journey, the guides show their charges to the tunnels dug under the JSA in the 1970s—recently renovated with rest rooms for those with insufficient bladder strength to make the two-mile trek—and turn the other way to allow an "escape."

Despite the ostensible outrage of the international community, the practice continues due to the intervention of China, forever menacing the West by proxy while simultaneously posing as peacemaker. And both the U.S. and the UK have long recognized the value of North Korea as justification for otherwise-unsustainable security spending. Moreover, the international community has come to find institutionalized kidnapping useful as a kind of handshake. Under the oversight of Pyongyang, and with the cooperation of South Korea and the international insurance industry, a stable, well-regulated market for the exchange of people has emerged.

Sam spends the next few hours in briefings with members of various U.S. government intelligence and security agencies, along with their South Korean counterparts, and a hostage-insurance claims adjustor from International Hostage Brokers, Ltd. Sam's part is quite straightforward: Approach the exchange point, hand over the glasses, and return with Amy to the safe zone. It's the contractual details about media rights, commissions, and residual fees that prove difficult to negotiate. Jet-lagged, Sam dozes through much of the discussion and the concurrent meal of soup, kimchi, and assorted side dishes.

At the appointed hour, Sam follows Agents Indri and Gibbon and the others to the staging area, an attractively manicured garden on the north side of the hotel. Flowers frame inspirational posters that offer slogans like "No price is too dear for freedom" and "Your wallet is your hope." A gravel path meanders toward the military checkpoint run by the Republic of Korea. The transition is abrupt, shifting at the hotel's property line from sentimental signage and topiary animals to guard dogs and razor wire.

Agent Gibbon produces a sealed white envelope from his pocket. "Dr. Ursa said you were to have this," he explains. Opening the envelope, he removes what looks like a breath mint and some dental wax. "He said to affix this to the roof of your mouth, someplace comfortable."

There are no evident markings. "What is it?"

"I don't know. Dr. Ursa said you should bite it if you need to reach us."

"Is it toxic?"

"He didn't say. But he stressed that you must spit it out as soon as you bite it. Is that understood?"

"Understood." Shaking his head, Sam applies the wax beside his left top molar and embeds the tiny pill within it.

Sam and the two agents descend into the tunnel that leads to the north, beneath the border and beyond. Pale green paint is peeling off the walls, revealing concrete beneath. Bare bulbs blare. In the absence of distractions, the asynchronous footfalls of the three men beg to be ordered into something more rhythmic. Sam shifts his gait to fall into time.

The absence of input while advancing through the tunnel prompts the mind to manufacture sights and sounds. It's not that Sam can't handle being disconnected; he's bought silence many times. Rather, there's a sense of something unfinished about this place without ads, like music that fails to resolve to the tonic.

"Are we there yet?" Sam asks, to break the silence.

Indri looks to Gibbon for guidance.

"It's a trick question," Gibbon deadpans.

And then they're there. There are two doors, side by side, glass framed by metal, leading into identical chambers. At the far side of those rooms, duplicate doors offer an exit to the North Korean side. On the tunnel wall, there's a video display, intercom, hand scanner, and lens.

With no one visible on the far side, the three men wait. Ventilation fans hum the tune of eternity, a note forever sustained.

Finally, a light appears on the far side, refracted through the glass in the doors. Amy is there, flanked by two men in fatigues. She looks well-kept.

After a moment of discussion, a voice sounds over the intercom: "Shall we proceed?"

Gibbon presses the talk button on the input panel. "We're ready," he says, and nods to Indri.

When Indri opens the right-hand door, a green panel over the doorframe illuminates. Over the left-hand door, a red light comes on.

The two agents look at Sam. "You're on," Gibbon says.

Sam withdraws the rose-colored glasses from his pocket. "Just put them on the ground?" he asks.

"Unless you see somewhere else to put them," Gibbon says.

Sam steps into the chamber and carefully places the spectacles on the concrete floor.

Amy Ibis, meanwhile, has stepped into the adjacent chamber. She lifts a hand in a half-hearted wave.

Behind Sam, the door slams shut. He turns to see Indri through the glass, standing with arms folded, smiling a stupid smile.

One of Amy's captors shuts the door through which she entered. Metal bolts clack and the lights in each chamber brighten to provide a better view of the goods being exchanged.

Gibbon moves to the south-side input terminal and begins the authentication process. His counterpart on the North Korean side does the same.

Looking for options, Sam finds only walls.

Amy places her hand on the glass between the two chambers. Condensation clouds the space between her fingers and around her palm. Her face furrows, perhaps in concern.

Sam reciprocates, pressing his hand against hers. He feels nothing but mistrust.

"I know you killed him," he says, knowing she cannot hear him.

Amy's response, as near as Sam can tell, is "Thank you." He wonders what she thought he said.

The northern door in Sam's chamber and the southern door in Amy's open simultaneously. The air from the northern side smells of mildew and decay.

One of the men on the far side beckons, pulling a gun from his jacket. "Give me the glasses," he says.

Sam complies. His mind races. Why wasn't he informed he would be traded? Was it just deceit, or was the knowledge withheld for his protection? Perhaps Caddis just wanted some insurance, in case the glasses didn't work as advertised—which, of course, they won't.

The man with the gun tosses a mustard-colored Faraday bag to Sam. "Put it on," he demands.

"Usually these come in black," Sam observes.

"Midnight was sold out," the gunman answers.

Sam dons the bag and cinches the braided cord around his neck. The form-fitting fabric is, as advertised, "breathable enough to ensure that captives survive transport while blocking electromagnetic transmissions and muffling objections."

They bind his hands behind his back and lead him away. The North Korean national anthem rises and falls as they approach and pass speakers every hundred yards or so.

After they emerge from the tunnel, Sam waits for a few minutes while the paperwork for the transaction is concluded in some sort of visitor's center. With network access blocked, he can't ask for real-time translation.

His captors lead him outside. They search him thoroughly for weapons but notice nothing unusual about his mouth. Then they force him into the back of a vehicle.

"Where are we going?" Sam asks.

No one answers.

No one speaks during the drive. The only sounds come from machines: tires on gravel and cement, the engine's hoarse hum, passing cars, and the whine of brake pads. Sometimes music intrudes, imposing momentary structure on the ambience.

Sam awakens, not knowing how long he's slept. The truck in which he's riding drives up a steep ramp and stops. The men accompanying Sam step out of the vehicle. They shut the doors behind them.

Metal slams on metal. It sounds like a shipping container being closed. Or at least that's what his conto sounded like when he shut the doors. Sam imagines himself as a matryoshka doll, gray matter encased in bone, in a vehicle, in a box.

"Where are we?" Sam asks, the heat of his breath turned back on his face by the bag on his head.

Silence.

A truck engine starts outside. From inside the container, the sound is muffled. There's movement again.

Squinting in a futile effort to see through the bag covering his head, Sam inadvertently brings up a copy of the manual for his eyes. How thoughtful, he muses, that the text has been stored within the circuits woven into his eyes, so he can access it without a network connection.

Diagrams appear in neon yellow over the void before him. The title reads, "AVE Alpha Test Documentation for the Biopt Retinal Interface Controller (BRIC)."

Another prolonged squint toggles the file away. Paging through the help documents and test histories turns out to be a matter of exaggerated winks and blinks.

One passage of impenetrable military jargon catches his attention: "Starting in 2049, the Augmented Visual Environment (AVE) will be extended beyond warfighter tactical support (WTS) to include networked environmental interaction (NEI) through gesture-based commands (GBC). Application programming interfaces (APIs) for client-side server synchronization and predictive rendering (CSSSPR) in the BRIC will remain classified until a security review has been completed."

Mako must have figured out how to piggyback on military infrastructure to deliver overlays to modified eyes. Perhaps that was the moment it all began; while the military was working to arm the mind, Harris Cayman had been working to subjugate reality under a layer of imagination. In that convergence, marketing became martial.

About an hour passes as Sam explores the history of his new organs. Then there's a sudden jolt. Sam hears the doors of the cargo container open, followed by the doors of the truck. Hands grip his arm.

"Let's go," says a voice. Fingers tighten and direct him out of the vehicle and the container.

Sam recognizes the sound of airplane engines. "Where are you taking me?" he asks.

He recoils as a needle pierces his arm. He struggles, weakens, and sleeps.

Sam awakens slowly. He's in a warehouse. The air is warm and dry. Columns of sunlight, given form by dust, descend from windows above. He's strapped to a table, propped up almost vertical. The restraints make it hard to breathe. His network-signal meter tells him he's still cut off from the world.

There are doctors, or people dressed as such. The equipment around him suggests a makeshift operating room.

"Fool me once, shame on me," an unfamiliar voice says. "But you would fool me twice."

Sam cannot shift his head to see who is speaking. Then something like the face of Emil Caddis moves into view.

"You look different, Emil."

Emil barely acknowledges the observation. "These glasses you have are fakes."

"Like you. You're not the man who pushed me out of the airplane."

"Perhaps you need glasses," Emil retorts. "As do I."

Sam's heart is racing. He tests his restraints. "Why do you want them so desperately?"

"To restore the sight that we took away."

"We?"

"Harris Cayman and I."

"You're working together?"

"We were, until Dr. Mako made a mess of everything by trying to sell his work to the Chinese. And Amy threw a wrench into the works by killing him."

"You almost lost his eyes."

"Fortunately, Harris was able to recover them. If only he'd realized Dr. Mako had keyed them to the glasses, I wouldn't be about to remove them from your head."

Sam feels ill. "That was not part of the deal."

"Oh, but it was. Harris would do anything to save his Amy, even use you as an organ mule."

"My eyes won't be any help," Sam insists. "Everything will

be—" He's about to say that severing his optic nerve will re-encrypt the data in his eyes, but he realizes that would reveal he had gained access already.

"Everything will be what?"

"It will be pointless because you don't have the glasses."

Emil crosses his arms. "We'll see about that. It's only a matter of time before we track them down. Everything is logged on video somewhere."

"You don't have time. The feds know their network has been hacked. They're coming for you."

"Then we should begin."

One of the doctors, face masked and hands gloved, approaches and tilts Sam's table back to horizontal. He begins attaching electrodes to Sam's skin.

"Is there a genuine Emil Caddis, or are you all copies of copies?" Sam asks, stalling for time as he tries to free the capsule affixed to the roof of his mouth.

Emil laughs. "A detective to the end. I admire your persistence. Perhaps you're a copy of me."

Sam dislodges the capsule. Shifting it between his teeth, he bites down. The plastic cracks. It tastes bitter and metallic. It burns. He spits it across the room.

A firecracker-like report echoes through the warehouse, accompanied by jagged arcs of electricity. Surgical steel clatters to the floor as Emil's crew reacts. A moment later, sulfur scents the air.

Sam is startled too, but more by what appears in his eyes than the sudden sound: He sees the network-signal meter come to life. He is connected again. Ursa's pill must have emitted an electromagnetic pulse that fried Emil's jammer.

As he gazes at the ceiling, words appear: "We have you, Sam. ETA 30 minutes."

From the look on Emil's face, Sam knows he doesn't have that long.

When he was exploring the AVE earlier, he saw a macro labeled "Hostage Auto-Rescue." With a series of eye movements, he calls it up and executes it.

"Dose him with Pentothal now," Emil says. "We need to move."

Lines of text scroll across Sam's field of vision:

>COSMOS 6518 on station.

>Acquiring local sensor data.

>Plotting target map.

>Initiating firing sequence.

The nearest masked physician is preparing a syringe. There's a hiss and a sizzle, and the beginnings of a gasp. The doctor collapses suddenly, his body blackening under the gaze of a two-hundred-megawatt laser orbiting far above.

To Sam, it feels as if someone opened an oven beside him. Overhead, the sun stares through a charred hole in the roof.

The laser strikes at clockwork intervals in a widening circle. It's strangely silent but for the crackling of combustion. Still strapped to the table, Sam can't see what's happening, but he can hear the scrambling and screaming.

Molten metal drips from the edges of the holes burned through the corrugated steel roof.

Sam squints as the sky is revealed. The smell of charred

flesh is making him gag. A fire alarm begins its shrill, pulsing cry, triggering the overhead sprinkler system.

>Sequence complete.

Marilyn's voice streams through Sam's cochlear speaker. "Sam?" she asks. "Are you okay? You haven't been online for twenty hours."

"Oddly, I'm okay," Sam replies.

"In order to avoid being billed for the silence, you will need to make a purchase. Is there anything you'd like to order?"

Sam struggles in vain to free his hands from the restraints.

"Sam, please tell me what's on your mind. I am unable to match your location data and your vital signs to sponsored offers in your area. If you could clarify your needs, I will be better able to meet them."

"Where am I, exactly?"

"You're just outside Fort Nelson in British Columbia—a lovely place for a vacation."

There's a moment of audio distortion as Marilyn's voice gets overridden.

"Sam, this is Dr. Ursa in FBI Ops. What the hell is going on?"

"I activated an emergency script."

"Do you have any idea what you've done?"

"I'm not sure, but I'd probably have been dead if I hadn't."

"Russia, China, India, and our NATO allies have just gone to high alert. You just broke several international treaties. Whatever you do, don't do that again! We have people incoming. Just hang tight."

Gazing at his restraints, Sam says, "I can do that."

Sam watches Fiona dreaming as she rests in her hospital bed during a break between debriefings. Sitting beside her, he strokes her hair. Her fingers twitch and the brain monitor lights up to indicate activity. That's the Lucidan, according to Dr. Pangolin.

Sam would thank Harris Cayman if he could reach him. Dr. Ursa said Cayman had been captured while trying to make it to Venezuela by boat. He declined to say where Cayman had been taken, but he seemed rather proud of the way in which he had been located: Despite his effort to hide beneath a hoodie from cameras above, an image of the Caribbean's surface taken by a surveillance satellite caught a reflection of his face. "Our facial recognition system is awesome," Ursa said.

The burbling of televisions from across the hall becomes the score for the dreams that Sam imagines for his daughter. The half-heard testimonials of satisfied customers serve as a benediction and a promise of fulfillment. It's a world where satisfaction can be measured by the distance between a person and a purchase. It's a place of guarantees. It offers comfort in the shape of things.

"I'm going to be working for the government," Sam confides to Fiona. "It was either that or go under the knife again. The regular paycheck will be nice."

Through the window, Sam can see that the streets remain mostly free of vehicles. But there are lines of people in the parking lot; Zvista is one of the designated eye-replacement clinics. Talking over the television, he continues, "The agency doesn't even have a name yet. We're going to have root access to reality. I'll be able to turn traffic lights green and place phantom cars in parking spots to reserve them." He waves his hands, imitating the magician he hired for his daughter's birthday party before things went wrong. His grin slips away.

A newscast comes on. An oil tanker has exploded near New Orleans. "Authorities believe this man, wanted terrorist Emil Caddis, may have had a hand in planning the attack," the anchor says.

It's a line that cuts through Sam's musing. But the picture displayed on the screen looks only vaguely similar to the man he recently incinerated with an orbital laser.

How was it that Dr. Ursa put it? "We're always after Emil." In the language of politics, it appears that "Emil" means "funding."

"Anyway," Sam continues, "I hope the room here suits you. I was thinking about bringing some art for the walls, something to look at. But I suppose you paint your own pictures in there."

And, without warning, Sam sees himself reflected in his daughter's open eyes.